D1485807

THE NEW WINDMILL SERIES

General Editors: Anne and Ian Serraillier

281

DEVIL BY THE SEA

DEVIL
BY THE SEA

Nina Bawden

HEINEMANN EDUCATIONAL BOOKS
LONDON

Heinemann Educational Books Ltd
22 Bedford Square, London WC1B 3HH

LONDON   EDINBURGH   MELBOURNE   AUCKLAND
HONG KONG   SINGAPORE   KUALA LUMPUR   NEW DELHI
IBADAN   NAIROBI   JOHANNESBURG
KINGSTON   PORT OF SPAIN

ISBN 0 435 12281 9

For

A.S.K. and T.R.F.

Printed and bound in Great Britain by
William Clowes Limited, Beccles and London

Chapter One

The first time the children saw the Devil, he was sitting next to them in the second row of deckchairs in the bandstand. He was biting his nails.

On the roof, the coloured flags cracked and streamed in the cold breeze from the sea but in the sheltered well of the bandstand it was warm and windless, the sun held the last heat of summer. Sleepy flies droned heavily over the sand scuffed on the flagstones by the children's feet. From time to time the blue sky split as an American jet plane screamed low.

The audience, this September afternoon, was made up of the very young, and the very old. The children, bright as butterflies in their summer dresses, filled the front rows of chairs; the old people huddled in rugs and scarves at the back, beyond the aisle. The local pensioners were issued with cheap season tickets by the council: wringing their last advantage from a mean world, they filled their seats at every performance.

Looking at the man sitting next to them, the children thought he must be old too, or sick. He wore a full-skirted naval bridge coat and a blue woollen muffler knotted round his neck. Beneath his cloth cap his face was thin, the cheeks so hollow that his mouth stuck forwards like a dog's mouth.

Grinning, Hilary nudged Peregrine with her elbow. She aped the man, tearing at the sides of her fingers with her teeth, rolling her eyes like a mad person. Peregrine watched her uncomfortably and then, as her acting grew wilder, he was seized by a fearful joy and laughed aloud.

The man turned and looked at them. A shadow crossed his face: like an animal, he seemed to shrink and cringe before the mockery Hilary had made of him. She stopped biting her nails and moved her hand nervously up her cheek and across her hair, pretending she had been brushing something from her face. He continued to watch her with a steady, careful stare. She fumbled in the pocket of her cotton dress. Her voice croaked with embarrassment.

"Would you like a toffee?"

The man looked beyond her, to Peregrine. Briefly, their eyes met. Peregrine could not look away, he was transfixed. The man's eyes were dark and dull, dead eyes without any shine in them. They reflected nothing.

The man stirred and coughed. His thin cheeks filled out and the spit sprayed from his mouth. "You're a nice little girl," he said, and smiled. It was a gentle smile, quite at odds with his appearance. He took a toffee with long, sharp fingers and popped it quickly in his mouth as if he were afraid it would be taken from him.

Hilary said, "Are you hungry? It must be awful to be hungry."

She was aware that it had been unkind to make fun of him. He could not help being sick and ugly. Normally, she did not suffer unduly for her bad behaviour towards other people unless she was punished for it. Her imagination was almost entirely absorbed by her own feelings which were, on occasion, bitter and terrible, and by the wild, dramatic happenings of her private world. But now her conscience was aroused by the man's sad and derelict air. Her heart swelled with pity.

"You can have them all if you're hungry. I don't want them."

She thrust the crumpled bag of sweets on to the man's

lap. His narrow, yellow face bent towards her. Reluctantly she looked up at the muddy eyes that showed nothing, neither hope nor despair nor love nor hate.

The man clicked his tongue against his teeth. "Are you sure you don't want them?"

She shook her head and lied, "I don't like toffees."

"What about your little brother?" Peregrine had withdrawn himself to another chair further along the row. He disliked embarrassing situations.

"They make his teeth wobble. He's just seven and all his teeth are falling out."

The man edged his chair closer to Hilary's. He smelt of wet mackintoshes like the cloakroom at school. Slowly his nervous tongue crept out of his mouth and slithered along his lips.

Hilary hunched herself small in her deckchair and watched the stage. Uncle Jack, the Kiddies' Friend, was making a bunch of flowers grow in an empty can. There was only one more trick after the can and then they would have the Children's Talent Competition. It was always held on a special day, the last day of the season. The Fun Fair would remain open for a little longer but after to-morrow there would be no more shows on the pier, the deckchairs would be hidden under their tarpaulin covers, the summer would be over. *The summer I was nine, thought Hilary. It will never come again. Next summer I shall be ten and then eleven and soon I shall be old. Soon, I shall die.*

The man was leaning closer still. His smell was in her nose and throat. She felt his hand stroking her knee and squirmed away. His fingers felt cold and hard like a chicken's foot. Ashamed, she stared at the stage, trying not to cry, pretending she hadn't noticed what he was doing.

Uncle Jack came to the front of the stage and smiled at the children, his perpetual, shining smile. He had stiff, curly hair like a doll. His teeth shone and his hair shone and he wore a great ring with a winking stone on the little finger of his left hand.

"Now, children, this is what you've been waiting for, isn't it? What? I can't hear you."

"*Yes*," bellowed the children with scarlet faces and straining lungs.

"That's better. *That's* better." He held up his hand for silence. "Those of you who have tickets, come up on to the stage. Gently, now. Don't all rush at once. You might knock me over."

There was a roar of laughter. A little girl sitting in front of Hilary stood up and skipped in front of her mother's chair. The woman creaked forward to pick up her canvas beach-bag, enormous, sun-reddened shoulders bulging out of her dress. She took out a green ticket.

"Here you are, Poppet. Now remember, stand up nice and straight and smile. . . ."

Poppet took the ticket. Over her mother's shoulder she smiled triumphantly at Hilary. She was very beautiful. She had fair, polished hair that bobbed on the shoulders of her green, satin dress. Her eyes were wide and blue like china; beneath her short skirt her long, brown legs looked like a miniature chorus-girl's. The man took his hand away from Hilary's knee. His teeth tore at his nails again.

Poppet jumped up on to the front of the stage. Her skirt flew up showing white frilly knickers with lace round the legs. Hilary saw them enviously. Her own knickers were voluminous, made of the same stuff as her dress and fastened with tight elastic.

Slowly, like the tide, the children flowed on to the stage. Some of them were shy: if they were little, Uncle Jack patted them on the head, if they were big he shook hands with them in a jolly, comradely way.

Hilary sighed. Screwing round in her chair, she looked for her half-sister, Janet. She saw her, standing by the entrance to the bandstand and talking to Uncle Aubrey. Waving her hands about in an affected way, she was quite preoccupied with her conversation. Her back was to the stage.

Hilary felt her heart pump inside her like an engine. She turned to her brother and said, "I'm going in the competition, too."

Blithely, he refused to believe her. "You haven't got a ticket."

She scowled. "I shall say I've lost it."

"That's wicked," he accused her. "It's a lie. God doesn't like us to tell lies."

Hilary saw the limpid light of Heaven shining from his eyes and hesitated. Peregrine was good: his goodness was as unquestioned as the rising sun. She knew him to be her spiritual superior and herself to be hateful and base.

She wriggled her shoulders and flung at him, "Mind your own business." She stood up and walked towards the stage, appalled by her own behaviour. Her legs seemed to be moving independently like someone else's legs. She could feel eyes sticking into her like hot spikes.

She stood in front of the stage and looked up at Uncle Jack. He saw a stout, pale-skinned child with red hair. Her nose was short and thick, her mouth was small and obstinate. Her plainness was redeemed by a bright, intelligent look which could be hidden at will beneath an expression of extreme stupidity. Uncle Jack held out his hand to her. "Come on, little lady, don't be frightened." His hand, soft and damp-skinned, grabbed at hers.

She said, prissy-mouthed, "I haven't got my ticket. I did have one, though. My sister bought it for me. I put it in the pocket of my frock but it fell out."

Uncle Jack stopped smiling and suddenly looked quite different, mean and wary. He looked much older when you were close to him, she decided. There was a faint-smear of what looked like face cream on the wrinkles at the corners of his eyes. He hesitated and pursed his lips.

"All right," he said, turning away, "go and join the others."

Hilary was bowed down with humiliation. She caught her lower lip between her teeth and blinked back her tears. From the stage, the bandstand looked enormous, row upon row of green and white striped deckchairs filled with pale, staring faces.

The accompanist struck a chord on the piano and the first child walked up to the microphone. He was very little, a tiny boy in crimson velvet trousers, and Uncle Jack had to shorten the stand as far as it would go. The boy wore glasses and his face was round and dark as a plum. His voice was gruff. His song began, "I'm too small to be in the infantry," and ended, "But I'm in the Lord's Armee."

The audience clapped through a wave of laughter. Uncle Jack bent down and asked him where he learned to sing the song. The little boy stared solemnly through his thick lenses and said, "Ford Road Mission."

There was more laughter and he was sent to the far side of the platform where he stood by the piano, sticking out his stomach and staring at the floor.

One by one, the children walked to the microphone. Four of them sang the same song, "How Much Is That Doggie in the Window?" Poppet was in front of Hilary. As she walked to the front of the stage, her skirt bumped on her little behind. She sang, "Lover Man," in a soft, husky, thread of a voice and swayed her hips in time to the music. When she had finished singing, she tap-danced, her skirt swirling high, her legs brown against her white knickers. The clapping was very loud and a group of big boys at the back of the audience whistled and stamped their feet.

Hilary took her place. Uncle Jack asked her name and announced it through the microphone. "What are you going to sing?" His teeth gleamed at her like a toothpaste advertisement.

"See Where Golden-hearted Spring."

It wasn't the kind of song that the other children had sung, but it was the only one she knew. She had learnt it, during the Easter term, for the Lent concert.

Uncle Jack patted her on the head and made a funny face. "Perhaps you'd like to tell them yourself," he said.

He adjusted the microphone and she spoke into it. Her voice, vast and booming, filled the bandstand. She saw Janet turn and look at her. She began to sing hurriedly, without the piano, forgetting to clasp her hands loosely in front of her but remembering to breathe deeply and sound her aitches even when there wasn't one at the beginning of a word. When she had finished the people clapped, only not as loudly as they had clapped for Poppet.

She stood unhappily by the piano and saw Janet's angry face across the line of deckchairs. She looked away from Janet and saw Peregrine. His shoulders were hunched, his thin legs twined miserably round the struts of the deckchair. She knew the depth of shame he must be feeling and longed to comfort him. Then she thought how generous and good she was to feel so sorry for him and, raising her eyes soulfully, stared at the sky.

The prizes were presented; a boy who had played the mouth organ was given ten shillings as the first prize and Poppet got five shillings for the second. All the children in the competition were given ice-cream cornets by Uncle Jack. They sat on the stage, eating their ice cream and watching the Punch and Judy show. Hilary kept her back towards the audience, her tongue lingering over the dry, sawdust taste of the cornet after the ice cream was gone. She had seen the Punch and Judy show several times that summer and during the performance she watched Poppet who was sitting beside her. One of the seams of Poppet's green dress had split. There was a tide mark on her neck and one of her front teeth was loose. She waggled it from time to time between her thumb and forefinger.

When the show was over Uncle Jack brought Mr. Punch out of his box to shake hands with the children and then he retired into a little room beside the stage where the conjuring things were kept.

Hilary said to Poppet, "I know Uncle Jack very well personally. I live here, you see, and he came to my Christmas party. He cost three guineas."

Poppet stared at her without speaking. Her beautiful oval face was pale and haughty. Hilary knew that she had committed a social blunder by speaking to her and her spirit shrivelled. Poppet tossed her head and, jumping lightly from the stage, ran to her mother. Lingering, Hilary saw them leave the bandstand and, as they left, the dirty man got up in a hurry and followed them.

Peregrine was waiting for Hilary. He said, pathetically, "You ate it all, every bit. It isn't fair. I didn't have an ice cream, did I?"

He looked very sad and small. She hardened her heart and reasoned with him. "You can't always have the same things as I do. It wouldn't be fair to me. I'm nearly ten."

He inquired hopefully, "When I'm three years older, will I be able to have more ice cream than you?"

"No, you won't. Because I'll still be older than you, even then. You'll never be as old as me, never, never." She spat the words gleefully into his face.

This was too much. His eyes grew large and miserable. "It's not fair."

She felt savage pleasure at his distress. She said with impatient cruelty, "You're greedy. God doesn't like little boys to be greedy."

She saw the bright tears glitter at the ends of his lashes. Pleased because she had hurt him, she became indulgent and maternal. She placed her arm round his shoulders and squeezed him affectionately. "I'll buy you a cornet," she promised generously. "On Saturday, when I get my pocket money."

Still conscious of injustice, Peregrine did not respond. "You get more pocket money than me, anyway," he said coldly and wriggled away from her.

Janet's voice startled them both. It rang out above their heads, loud and angry.

"What on earth do you think you were doing? Wait till we get home, you'll catch it." There were red patches on her neck, she grabbed at the children's hands.

Hilary said in a high, carrying voice. "I went in for the competition. I know I didn't have a ticket. I pretended I'd lost it."

Janet glanced hastily round her and said in a low, entreating voice, "Hilary, *do* be quiet. Do you want everyone to know?"

Hilary sensed, behind the reprimand, Janet's basic dislike of her. She looked beyond Janet, at the man standing awkwardly behind her and said pointedly, "It's not my fault. You didn't try to stop me, did you? Mummy said you were to look after us but you didn't. You were too busy talking." Her face smarted with incipient tears.

Janet glared at her vengefully and chewed her lower lip. Uncle Aubrey laughed. Bending down, he spoke to Peregrine. "Didn't you want to be in the competition, old chap?"

"No thank you," Peregrine answered politely. He was always polite, a graceful child. He seemed to know instinctively what grown-up people wanted of him and as a result they adored him. He looked so sweet, too, in his blue, Dayella knickers and striped shirt. His face was pale and narrow with delicate bones, his straight, blond hair and soft brown eyes gave him a wistful, orphaned look. His ears stuck out almost at right angles to his head and were the source of much ridicule. At school, the bigger boys pulled him along by them. He was not popular with other children: they thought him smug and stuck up. Only Hilary knew he was not. She knew he was painfully shy and genuinely good, and longed to please everyone.

Now he continued to smile with great sweetness and to regard Janet and Aubrey with a fixed and aimiable stare. Hilary wondered if he knew they were in love. She found it difficult to believe that they were for Janet was not pretty: her nose was too big, her hair never curled and her skin was brown as a gypsy's. She was too ugly to be loved and yet, watching them from behind a rock one long, hot afternoon, Hilary had seen them kiss each other.

Janet said, "Would you like to go on the beach for a little while? We haven't to go home yet."

Hilary sniffed. "It'll be cold on the beach. But we'll go if *you* want to. Can we go by the pier?"

"If you like," Janet answered coldly and held out her hand to Peregrine.

Outside the bandstand, the wind blew keenly. The beach was almost empty, a wide, shingly waste, and beyond the shingle, stretching to the creaming edge of the sea, was the shining blue mud and the slippery rocks with the gulls crying over them. There was the smell of low tide; the faint, pervasive smell of worms and snails and jellyfish and crabs; the lovely iodine smell of seaweed left drying by the ebbing sea.

Peregrine walked between Janet and Aubrey. They each held one of his hands and swung him in great leaps over the cracked paving-stones. He laughed and they smiled self-consciously at each other above his head. Behind them, Hilary trailed her feet along the pavement, her face fixed in a mutinous scowl. She saw Poppet and her family sitting in the shelter of the jetty and tugged at Janet's skirt.

"I want to go there." She pointed.

"Not on the pier? For heaven's sake, make up your mind." Janet turned to Aubrey with an expression that said, "See what I have to put up with?" She gave a false, merry laugh. "A frightful child. Never knows her own mind from one minute to the next."

For form's sake, Hilary said to Peregrine, "Come and throw stones in the sea." When he shook his head, she did not try to persuade him and, alone, crunched across the shingle towards the jetty. Poppet's mother was leaning back in a deckchair with her eyes closed. Two little boys played beside her, aiming stones at a bucket. Poppet had climbed across the jetty and was building a hill of stones on the other side. There were very few people on the beach.

Hilary peered across the jetty at Poppet. Then she saw the man who had been sitting next to her in the bandstand. He was standing by the steps that led from the promenade to the beach, quite close to where Poppet was playing.

Hilary leaned against the angle of the sea wall and the jetty and closed her eyes. She felt that she looked pale and distinguished. Perhaps Poppet would notice her and say, "How ill you look, would you like to play with me? We could go by ourselves to the Fun Fair and spend my prize money." Hilary would suggest that they took Peregrine with them and Poppet would laugh and say they didn't want boys. They weren't any good at anything, were they? I'll count twenty very slowly, she said to herself, and when I open my eyes she'll come and speak to me. She closed her eyes tightly and began to count. When she opened them, nothing had happened except that the sky was clouding over above the houses on the cliff.

Poppet had not moved but the man was squatting beside her now, the skirts of his long coat spread out on the shingle. They were talking. Once, he flung up his arm and pointed towards the pier.

Hilary sat down and watched the two younger children. They took no notice of her. She stared at them, willing them to look at her. She picked up a stone and threw it at their bucket. It missed the bucket and hit one of the little boys on the leg. He wailed, his mother opened her eyes and said automatically, "Mind what you're doing, now."

The little boy snivelled and wiped his nose on his sleeve. He picked up his bucket and toddled down the shelving beach to the end of the jetty where he stood, weeping and resigned, ankle-deep in the yellow foam left behind by the retreating tide.

Sighing deeply, Hilary stood up and climbed on to the jetty. She had to lean on her chest and pull her legs up sideways. Lying flat on the slimy, smelly surface, she saw Poppet stand up and take the man's hand. They walked together up the steps and on to the promenade. The man's cloak blew about him, he looked like a great, black bird.

Hilary dragged herself upright on the jetty, scraping her knees, and watched them go. The sky was dark now, a flat, dull, metal colour. She jumped down on the other side of the jetty and behind her, his voice made thin and fading by the wind, Peregrine called, "Hilary, Hilary, wait for me."

Peregrine had not wanted to go on the beach. He was cold, the wind brought out goose pimples on his skin and the tips of his fingers had gone white and bloodless. He did not complain, he had learned to accept the discomforts of a bad circulation, but when Janet and Aubrey sat on the edge of a beached boat he stood beside them, frowning in a reproachful manner until Janet, giving his shoulder a quick, impatient push, said, "Run along, dear, do."

When he had gone, Aubrey at once resumed the conversation that had been interrupted by the end of the children's performance. He had been waiting impatiently to do so: he loved the sound of his own voice. Sheltering the flame with his jacket, he struck a match and lit his pipe. The words emerged muffled through clenched teeth. "As I was saying, Janet, I can't possibly disassociate myself from Milly's problem. I see it so pathetically clearly. Perhaps more clearly because I don't love her. She is utterly dependent on me. . . ."

He stared reflectively at his pipe. The spent match hissed on the wet stones. His profile was stern and affecting. "I don't mean just socially and economically. The important thing is that she needs me mentally. I think for her, I am her *mind*." He gestured sombrely at the wide horizon. "Sometimes I think that I did her an injustice in marrying her. If she had had to continue alone, she might have become a more complete *person*." He emphasised the word, "person" lovingly, as if it had a very special significance. He continued, "As it is, if I were to leave her now, she would be lost. A foreigner in a strange land without a phrase book. A foreigner who didn't know a word of the language," he amended gravely, always pedantically anxious to make himself clear.

Ignoring the thrill of fear and joy that shot through her at the thought of Aubrey leaving his wife, Janet said tartly, "I thought you married her because she said she was pregnant."

He turned wide, surprised eyes towards her. He was

wounded by her vulgarity. "Janet," he said, with infinite, sad reproach, "Oh, Janet."

"I'm sorry," she mumbled. Her eyes veiled, she plucked at a sticky burr that was tangled in the wool of her jersey.

There was a silence. Then his arm crept round her shoulders and he said, in a deep, rich, loving voice, "Janet, my poor child. It's my fault. I should never have talked to you about Milly. It was tactless of me."

This sentiment put her completely in the wrong.

"Oh, no," she protested eagerly. "Of course we must talk about her."

The wind caught his light-brown hair and swept it into agreeable disorder, hiding the patch of baldness on his temple that occasionally distressed her. He was a handsome young man with a profile that distracted women, a thin mouth and cold, angry eyes.

She repeated earnestly, "It's awfully important that you should tell me what you really *feel*. That sort of thing is more important between a man and a woman than anything else. More important than sex."

She brought out the last word with difficulty and lowered her eyes. She thought, with a stirring of pride, that six months ago she would not have dared to mention that word to a man. She remembered Miss Adams, the botany mistress, whose neck had become as red as a hen's whenever she was forced, by the nature of the curriculum, to approach the "difficult subject".

Aubrey smiled approvingly at her and she leaned her head comfortably against his shoulder. His beautiful, deep, rich voice droned on and Janet contemplated the poetic tragedy of her own position. She was in love with a married man. This did not make her unhappy. Indeed, in the beginning, it had given their love an additional piquancy, a spice of danger. "Illicit love," she had frequently said to herself in the privacy of her bedroom, "Illicit love." The words had a brave and glorious ring.

They had met, earlier in the year, on the beach. They had paddled in the cold, spring sea, talked and gathered shells just—as Aubrey had said himself—like a couple of children. He was a schoolmaster and these summer holidays they had met almost daily. They talked—Janet had never talked so much, nor known there were such interesting depths in her own character—and occasionally Aubrey read his own poetry to her.

Their relationship had been, in Aubrey's words, as fresh and innocent as a spring morning. They were not lovers although the question whether they should one day become so, had often been discussed between them. At least, Aubrey had discussed it: unable to emulate his detachment or to speak of sex without embarrassment (in the Sixth Form, such talk would have been dismissed as "sloppy") Janet had meekly listened. He had attacked the matter both from a moral and a psychological standpoint. It was the effect on *her* that worried him, he frequently said: women were more disposed than men to be emotionally affected by the physical act. At first Janet had been touched by his consideration but lately his reflective monologues had ceased to excite and merely bored her. So much talk about what should be a spontaneous and fleshly business must inevitably lead to disappointment. Desire was bound to wither in this earnest, debating-society atmosphere. Now, drowsily listening to his voice, she decided that by the time she became Aubrey's mistress, all the fun would have gone out of it.

Her own cynicism appalled her. She sat upright and said fervently, "I love you so much."

"What?" Interrupted in his monologue (what, she wondered guiltily, had it been about?), Aubrey's voice was brusque. He recovered himself quickly. "Do you?" His eyes wandered over her hair. "Sometimes I wish you didn't. It would be easier for me to love you from a distance. Knowing that I could never have you." He smiled beautifully. "*La Princesse Lointaine*," he murmured. "Cold and pale and virginal."

Not for the first time, Janet found him absurd. He's rehearsing a scene with some quite imaginary person, she thought. Seeing the impatience in her eyes, Aubrey blushed faintly and pressed his lips against her cheek.

On the beach, a child wailed. Looking up, they saw that a small boy had fallen in a pool by the jetty. He was standing in the water, soaked to the skin, the tears pouring down his outraged face. His mother left her deckchair and lumbered down to the pool.

"Where are the children?" said Janet.

They stood up. On either side, as far as they could see, the beach was empty.

"They can't have gone far," Aubrey said.

Janet tossed her head at him and ran clumsily towards the steps, head bent, slipping on the stones. From behind she looked angular and coltish; her shrunken cardigan barely reached below her shoulder blades. She stood on the promenade breathing asthmatically, puffed by her run.

When Aubrey caught up with her, she turned a distracted face towards him. "They might be anywhere," she cried. "We should have watched where they went. They might have gone near the road."

He thought her distress excessive. Looking at his watch, he saw that he would be expected at home. "Surely they can't have gone far?"

Irritated by his calm, she said, "Don't worry yourself, will you? I'll find them, you go home." Seeing he was quite prepared to do just this, she added spitefully, "It's all your fault. You knew I was supposed to look after them."

Her unfairness astonished him. He took revenge by observing, coldly and silently, that anger made her nose more prominent and her skin more sallow. Really, her only beauty lay in an awkward, young simplicity and bloom: she should be more conscious of her limitations and understand that to be sweet and continuously charming was her only hope. But however vicious his private thoughts, Aubrey was too cautious to speak them aloud. He did not love Janet but he had literary ambitions and believed that an *affaire* was necessary to an aspiring young writer. He had no intention of making Janet his mistress but in the absence of anyone more stimulating she was a useful object on which to practise his technique. He said mildly, "Perhaps they have gone on the pier."

She muttered, "They haven't got any money. It costs twopence." Irresolute, angry with herself, she turned on him. "We just sat and talked and talked," she cried in wild despair. "We were only thinking of ourselves. Anything might have happened to them."

When Peregrine called to her, Hilary hesitated for a moment. Then she saw that Poppet and the man had stopped at the telescope. The man put a penny into the slot, Poppet climbed on to the platform and looked through the eyepiece. Then she got down and, hand in hand, the man and the child walked on, towards the pier.

Hilary glanced at Peregrine, labouring over the clattering shingle, his face purple in the wind. She decided that she wouldn't wait for him: it would teach him a lesson.

She climbed the steps to the promenade and hurried to the telescope to see if there was anything left of the pennyworth but the shutter at the end had already clicked down. Anyway, there was nothing to look at. Where the telescope was pointing, there were no boats, nothing but the wide and empty sea.

She skipped along the front, past the clock tower and the lavatories, stopping at the photographer's kiosk to pat the old, stuffed bear that stood outside. Some of his inside was coming out and one eye was missing. Sometimes there was a queue of children waiting to have their pictures taken sitting on the bear but this afternoon it was too cold, there was no one there. She inserted a finger into the worn hole on the bear's back and pulled out a little more of the kapok stuffing. Then she saw that the photographer was watching her thoughtfully from his little box: she hummed a casual tune under her breath and ran on.

A little farther along the front, you came to the pier and the Fun Fair and beyond that the town petered out into the flat marshes of the estuary where once the herons had nested and now there was nothing except a road, protected by the high, sea wall, a few wooden shacks and the soft, flat land crumbling away before the encroaching sea.

Poppet and the man had stopped outside the Fun Fair. They were looking into the distorting glass that hung outside the entrance to the fair, advertising the Hall of Mirrors, the Big Laugh. The little girl was pointing to her reflection in the mirror. The sound of her high, light laugh came to Hilary on the wind.

Hilary walked a little closer and stood in a prominent position so that if they turned round, they would see her. If they were going into the Fun Fair and saw another little girl, alone, perhaps they would take her too. She saw that Poppet was pulling at the man's hand, almost as if she wanted to get away, but he was bending over her protectingly, sheltering her with his great, black coat. His attitude was one of loving kindness.

Suddenly, for no reason at all, Hilary was afraid. The whole sea front was cold and empty and dead, her heart beat loudly. She no longer wanted to be seen: she bolted into the doorway of a café and hid behind a placard that said "Oysters in Season". The wording of the notice was hopeful but faded and dim. No one who came to Henstable would be likely to ask for oysters. The café did a brisk trade in fish and chips and Coca-Cola. With relief, Hilary saw that Peregrine was running along the front towards her.

His hair streamed behind him, the tears were drying on his cheek. "Why didn't you wait for me?" he panted accusingly. "I didn't hear you," she lied softly. His hands, she saw, were white with cold. "Give them to me," she commanded and he yielded them meekly so that she could rub them between her knuckles.

"Why did you go without me?" he complained. "What are you doing here? Are you hiding from someone?"

"Be quiet," she hissed, thumping him warningly between the shoulder blades. Apprehensive, he followed the direction of her eyes.

The man and the little girl had left the entrance to the Fun Fair and were walking away from the town, towards the marshes. They were linked closely together as if a great affection bound them. From this distance it was impossible to tell whether the child's steps were lagging or whether she went willingly. Once she turned round, her small face, as flat and blank and meaningless as a piece of white paper, appearing briefly against the man's dark sleeve. Perhaps she was crying: if she was, it was a very tiny cry, not loud enough to be heard above the sound of the sea and the noisy yelling of the gulls. The man's wide skirts blew around them both so that some of the time Poppet was almost completely hidden. She was so small, now, that she had little character or significance. She was, already, a committed child, lost beyond redemption.

The children, sensing that something irrevocable was happening, drew closer together and watched in silence.

At last Hilary whispered, "I wonder where they're going." Peregrine did not answer her. He was breathing noisily, watching the departing couple with a fixed, glazed stare.

Hilary said hopefully, "I expect he's her Daddy." This, on the whole, had not seemed likely so she tried again. "Or her Uncle, or somebody like that."

Peregrine suddenly flushed bright scarlet. "He's not anyone she knows. He's taking her away. He's the Devil."

As he spoke, the colour ebbed from his face as quickly as it had come, leaving him very pale. He took a pace forward, one hand clutching Hilary's wrist. Memory served him now, not sight, for the figures had dwindled. He remembered what he had seen, without understanding, when the man had sat beside him in the bandstand: the clumsy horror beneath the full, concealing skirts, the surgical boot, the club foot. Now he knew what he had seen and felt the knowledge strike him like a sword.

"He's the Devil," he insisted gently. "I saw . . ." He caught his breath and began to cry. "I saw his cloven hoof."

Hilary felt quite faint and sick. Peregrine was always truthful. She remembered the Nanny who had said long ago when they were in their bath to an aunt or some other, shadowy, forgotten figure, "That child's a saint, too good to live. He'd never tell a lie, not to save his soul." Then, the wraith-like person, swathed in steam and bath towels, had muttered something about long ears and no more had been said.

That night, lying awake in the moon-cold nursery, Hilary had thought that Peregrine was going to die or, worse, had somehow damned himself irretrievably, and sobbed herself to sleep. When morning came and she watched Peregrine across the breakfast table, saw his calm, living face, this acute terror passed and she knew that the sly words had been no more than a cold dig at *her*, Hilary, the untrustworthy one, the unwanted girl, the liar. From that moment she had known that she was wicked and worthless and that Peregrine was wholly good, the beloved of God, the flower of the flock.

If Peregrine said that he had seen the Devil, it was true. He knew the Devil when he saw him because he was a saint, too good to live. With a bursting heart, she cried, "Let's go back, go back. . . ." She began to run, weeping, into the wind. After a little, her breath gave out and she turned to Peregrine. "You're quite sure?" she asked.

"Oh yes." His clear eyes looked back at her with tranquil certainty. He was no longer troubled by his vision. He believed in the Devil and, after the first shock, to see Him had seemed nothing out of the ordinary.

He said calmly, "Let's play at jumping over the cracks, shall we?"

Slowly, hopping and skipping, they returned to the jetty. Janet was standing by the clock tower alone, looking in the opposite direction. Giggling, they slipped down on to the beach and crept along in the shelter of the sea wall.

The face of Poppet's mother appeared above the jetty. There was a spot on her chin, an inflamed, red pustule with a fat, white head.

"Poppet," she called. She ignored the children and her voice was squeaky as if she were angry or afraid. "Poppet, come here this minute."

She clambered on to the jetty, flopping on her forearms like an old seal as she heaved her legs sideways. Her cotton skirt whipped in the wind. Her legs were knotted with purple veins and thick as tree trunks. She wore dirty, white plimsolls, the laces dangled. Hilary watched her, thinking how ugly she was. Beside her, Peregrine turned his face away. He found ugliness quite unbearable, it made him sick.

"Poppet."

The salt wind tore at the dry, permed hair. Legs straddled wide, she stood on the slimy jetty and looked wildly at the empty beach, at the grey, curling sea.

"Hilary, you naughty girl. I've been looking everywhere."

Janet bore down upon them like an avenging angel. She seized Hilary's hand and pulled her towards the steps, prodding Peregrine in front of them. Hilary dragged back, watching the woman over her shoulder.

"How *could* you? I've been out of my mind. Don't you ever think of anyone except yourself?"

Janet's voice was quivering, her breast heaved beneath her cotton dress.

"I'm sorry," Peregrine said instantly, his mouth trembling.

"Oh, it's not your fault. I'm not cross with *you*," Janet said contemptuously. She waited, her face bent wrathfully towards her little sister. Hilary could never apologise. Sometimes she wanted to but the words always stuck in her throat like pills. Now, sullenly staring at her sandalled feet, she tried to distract attention from this failing in her character.

"It wasn't my fault, either. I saw the Devil."

She smiled proudly at Janet, confident that this was excuse enough. What else she had seen was too terrible to think of for the moment, too private to mention.

"This is too much. . . ."

The words, exploding like rifle shots, the tone of utter exasperation, came as a surprise to Hilary. She looked up, puzzled.

"But it's true. Peregrine saw him, too."

Wordlessly, Janet turned towards Peregrine. His uplifted face expressed a deep, inner calm.

"Well?" asked Janet.

He shook his head. He could not speak. He knew, already what Hilary could never learn; what was acceptable to the grown-up world and what was not. Only Nanny would have understood; it was Nanny who had formed his beliefs in a personal, vengeful religion; Nanny who, more than anything else, had meant security and safety and home. But Nanny had left in a huff one hot, August morning; she had kissed him, called him her lamb and her love, reminded him to remember, always, his prayers. "Though how long you'll be allowed to in this heathen house is more than the Dear Lord knows," she had finished, wiping the tears from her cheek with her cracked, leather glove, turning away, leaving him for ever.

Now, if he were to back Hilary up as he knew he should, Janet would only say it was that awful woman putting ideas into his head. He could not bear anyone to attack Nanny. He had been even less able to bear it since her departure because he could no longer make it up to her by climbing on her lap and kissing her rough, scrubbed cheek. Whereas he could compensate Hilary in a hundred different ways. He could let her have some of his things. Nothing that belonged to Hilary ever worked for five minutes together and usually Peregrine was careful not to lend her anything he valued because, once lent, it was gone for ever. But now, as he'd let her down, he would give her anything she wanted, even his ball-point pen. But would she think even the sacrifice of his pen enough? Would she spurn the rich gift, turn from him with loathing? The conflict of loyalties tore him in two: it was like a death.

Janet, watching him, thought he looked tired and washed out. "There," she said triumphantly to Hilary, "you've been filling him up with a lot of nasty stories."

"I have not." She stamped her foot. "He saw the Devil too. He *did*. And so did I. He's just lying." She glared at Peregrine. Before her angry eyes, his own shifted and fell. "Liar," she said pungently, and he began to snivel.

"That's enough." Janet jerked Hilary's arm so hard that

it hurt her shoulder. "Come along, or we'll miss the bus. Run, Hilary, or are your legs too fat?"

They ran. The cold wind whipped their hair. The bus was waiting. They sat on the upper deck, Janet and Peregrine in the front seat. Janet's arm was laid affectionately round Peregrine's shoulders. Hilary looked at them and longed for Janet to love her.

She said, "We might have got lost while you were talking to Aubrey. Mummy would have been angry with you."

"Shut up," said Janet, without turning her head.

"Do you love Aubrey, Janet? You can't marry him, you know, he's married already."

Janet stared out of the window. The bus started with a jolt and moved along the front. Hilary looked at the sea and saw, on the lonely beach, the woman stumbling along the shingle, one child tucked under her arm and hoisting her skirt above her knee, the other trailing behind. Above her, the gulls whirled and screamed against the stormy, metal-coloured sky.

Hilary shivered and looked away. She gazed at her transparent reflection in the glass of the window. "Janet," she said, in a coaxing voice, "will you take us to the Fun Fair before we go back to school?"

Chapter Two

Charles Bray, the children's father, sat in the stuffy cubby-hole at the back of his shop with a cup of tea and the evening paper and hesitated to telephone his wife. If he telephoned her, she would laugh at him and he was afraid of her laughter.

The face of the murdered child stared up at him from the badly printed page. She had lost one of her milk teeth and the gap gave her face a sentimental innocence that her eyes denied. They were bright eyes with a clear, knowing look: she was a very self-conscious little beauty. Dressed in her party frock, she had posed for the camera artfully, turning slightly away so that you could see the childish line of her cheek, the loveliness of bone beneath the baby flesh. He saw, briefly, what she might have grown into: the pretty blonde from the London slum, a rose in the gutter, the boys mad about her. Her name had been Camelia, Camelia Perkins. Wondering what wild and hopeless fantasy had inspired her christening, he thought the grand name made her ugly death seem even more pointless and absurd, a kind of cosmic joke.

He stubbed out his cigarette and swore at himself. He was being foolish. Death had given this sad child no significance: it had only finished the promise of those eyes. She was not important any more. Only the living mattered, his children with a madman loose in the town. His panic mounted. He stretched out his hand and slowly dialled the number of his house.

The telephone rang once and Alice answered it. "Is anything the matter, dear?"

"You're not busy?" he inquired nervously. She was frequently impatient when he telephoned her: her day, she sometimes hinted, was a good deal more fully occupied than his.

"No, dear. I've just had a bath."

He pictured her, sitting at her dressing-table, talking into the white, telephone receiver and watching herself in the glass.

He said flatly, "You remember that child who was missing two days ago? The little girl?"

"Have they found her?"

"In one of those filthy huts on the flats. She was murdered."

"How dreadful," she said in an interested, bright voice. "Is it all in the papers?"

"Yes. In the evening papers. Alice . . ." He cleared his throat. "Are the children home?"

He heard her chuckle softly. "No, Charles. They're on the beach. But nothing can happen to them. They're with Janet, quite safe."

"I suppose Janet is responsible?" A new worry nagged his mind. "You know what young girls are. Running about after boys."

"Not Janet, dear. She's a nice, sheltered, hockey-playing schoolgirl. She knows nothing about sex except what she learned in Botany."

"Perhaps you're right. She doesn't mind looking after the children, does she?"

There was an edge to her voice. "Why should she? When *I* was seventeen, I'd been earning my living for three years. And looking after an invalid mother."

"I know, dear. I'm sorry." He felt deeply guilty about his

wife's early life. She had had a terrible childhood and he could not bear to think about it. She had only to mention it to gain the moral advantage in any disagreement between them.

Alice went on, "Now, Charles, you must promise me not to worry over the children. They'll be home quite soon. I'll telephone you if you like. But you mustn't get worked up for nothing. It's bad for you."

Her voice, indulgent and reproving, set his teeth on edge. The blood rushed to his forehead. "Do you call murder nothing? It seems to me . . ."

The door of his cubby-hole opened and Miss Hubback, his assistant, peered at him inquiringly. He beckoned her in and she squeezed past his desk to the pile of school atlases that were stacked in the corner. She was a heavily built young woman whose drooping breasts, beneath a nylon blouse, were inadequately enclosed in a pink, spotted brassiere. The effect was neither provocative nor pretty. As she bent over the atlases, Charles saw an expanse of fat, pale thigh. One of her stocking seams was twisted. Charles averted his eyes.

Alice said patiently, "What were you going to say, dear? *Must* you say, 'it seems to me'? It's becoming such a silly habit." He knew that her face had assumed a sweet, martyred expression. "Now, Charles, I'm just as worried as you are. You know how terribly I worry over the children. But I *force* myself to control it. For their sakes. It's so bad for them to feel that you're worried on their behalf. It destroys their sense of security."

Miss Hubback tiptoed elaborately back to the shop. Before she closed the door she smiled at Charles brightly, showing her strong teeth.

Alice continued, "So you're not to be a silly old hen. Think of your blood pressure. The children won't be long. I'll go and watch for the bus as soon as I've made myself

35

decent. And I'll let you know the moment they're safely home. Will that do?"

"Yes," he said. "That'll do. Thank you." He wondered why he was thanking her. Perhaps because it was nice of her to humour him.

He said, "I'm sorry if you think I'm being an ass."

"Not an ass, darling. Just an old fussbudget. But I love you."

It was only a gesture, he thought, a habit, like asking people how they were when really you didn't care at all.

He said, "I love you, too," and put the telephone down. He was conscious of feeling tired, the way he had often felt tired lately when he had been talking to Alice. It was as if an enormous physical effort had been asked of him and his body had to call upon all its reserves of energy. He longed for peace.

It was odd, he thought, because Alice wasn't particularly difficult. She was a good sort and she didn't nag, except very occasionally. And anyway, he loved her. He must hang on to that: he loved his wife.

He looked at the letter lying on his desk and the murder went out of his mind. His rates had been put up in the last assessment: they were three times what they had been when he had taken over the bookshop at the end of the war. As things stood at the moment, to pay them would just about cripple him. He supposed he could appeal: he wondered what good it would do. He brushed his hand over his eyes and thrust the demand into an open drawer among the other unpaid bills. He would think about it to-morrow. He got up heavily and went into the shop.

Replacing the receiver, Alice smiled at herself in the glass. Charles was getting to the difficult age, she thought, he took everything so hard. If he wasn't worrying about the children, he was worrying about his health or about the business. He walked through life suspiciously, beset by imaginary dangers on every side.

She picked up a brush and painted her lips carefully. The silver charms tinkled on the bracelet on her wrist. Her raised, bare arm was shapely, the flesh smooth and covered with freckles. As she outlined her eyes with a dark pencil, she thought about the murder and about the empty field behind the house, dense with long grass and scrubby thorn bushes. It had been bought by a speculative builder at the beginning of the summer and he was waiting for his licence. Anyone could approach the back of the house without being seen. Perhaps there was already someone there, waiting and watching.

The pulse jumped in her throat. Her wide, alarmed eyes stared back at her from the tinted mirror. How silly and thoughtless of Charles to alarm her so. He knew how imaginative she was. . . .

She stood up and regarded herself critically in the glass, her lips pursed. The grey dress fitted her perfectly, the soft wool flowed easily over her breasts and hips. She was a big woman and needed to dress carefully. She twisted round to see that her stocking seams were straight and touched her braided hair. A small, pleased smile flickered on her lips.

She left her bedroom and went slowly down the stairs. A floor creaked and her heart raced. Muttering under her breath, she went into the kitchen, shut and bolted the back door. The action stirred up panic: she ran from room to room, closing and locking the windows against the chill air of the dying summer. She stood in the hall, her hand to her heart, listening to the ticking of the clock.

The stillness came alive around her. Whispering sounds menaced her from every room. Perhaps she had locked the door too late, perhaps there was already someone in the house? She was alone except for Auntie, resting in her room. And Auntie, Charles's Aunt Florence, would never have heard an intruder: she was deaf as a post. Intractable, old and proud, she refused to admit this failing of her senses although for years she had heard no sounds but the ringing bells inside her own head.

Thinking of this, an ancient resentment stirred. Why should Auntie be allowed to keep her eccentric illusion just because her father had been a knight? Anger drove out fear.

"Don't be a bloody fool," Alice said aloud. She never swore in public, being anxious, above all things, to appear well bred, but when she was alone she frequently abused herself with violent expressions and found they comforted her. "You silly, neurotic bitch," she said. The sound of her voice pleased and calmed her. Her pulses resumed their normal, regular beat.

Glancing at her watch, she left the house and walked to the front gate, looking across the Downs to the wide sea. Peebles was one of a single line of houses built high on the cliff top with an uninterrupted view of the sea and, in summer, of the long line of yellow sewage that appeared, bubbling beyond the outer limits of the tide. The road was called The Way. The houses were big and rambling, Gothic in conception: at the time of their construction they had been thought rather grand houses. When Alice had been a child, the road had been a fashionable place to live. The best people in Henstable lived on The Way: at Christmas-time, the best parties had been given there and they were always the parties Alice had not been invited to. She used to walk up and down the road after dark, an angry child, loving and hating the people in the houses, watching the lighted windows and listening to the laughter. That was how she was always to feel: the good things happened on the other side of the wall.

Now the grandeur of the houses had diminished. They were merely large and inconvenient and shabby, the gardens impossible to maintain. They expressed, in their peeling paint, their dusty chandeliers, a whole chapter of middle-class decay. There were no more parties. The only rich household left belonged to Miss Fleery-Carpenter and she was old, potty, lived on boiled onions and the daily expectation of the Second Coming of Christ. Apart from the Brays, the owners of the houses were old, mostly retired people, barely conscious, though they discreetly let rooms in summer and grumbled about rising prices, that the world had changed. Occasionally they would remark to each other that people "of their sort" did not live in Henstable any more.

But to Alice Bray, who had been Alice Parker, the bright, disciplined child from the slum houses at the other end of the town, it still seemed, for most of the time, a considerable achievement to be living on The Way. She, who had run the streets, been beaten by a drunken father, been abandoned by him at the age of fourteen, left in sole care of a paralysed, whining mother, now owned a car, sent her children to expensive schools, voted Conservative.

Smiling and well-nourished, she stood at the gate of her comfortable, shabby house and looked down the hill towards the town. From where she stood she could see the beach, the flags on the roof of the bandstand, and the long finger of the pier pointing out to sea. The sea was calm and blue, the blue sky swept down to meet it: it was a beautiful day.

As she watched, a tiny, toy bus left the pier and crawled slowly along the front. It was the four o'clock bus, the one the children usually caught when they had been on the beach. In a moment or two it would reach the foot of the hill and she could telephone Charles, tell him that the children were safe and go out to tea.

39

She hoped that the children had heard nothing of the trouble in the town. She must warn Janet to say nothing to them. Peregrine would not understand what had happened but Hilary was precocious and excitable: she would see at once the dramatic possibilities in the situation and use them to the full. Once she knew about the murder, she would be impossible for weeks.

The bus stopped at the bottom of the hill. She saw Janet and the children get out, three small, distant figures in cherry-coloured cardigans. She went into the house.

Miss Hubback answered the telephone. She sounded breathless. "Oh, it's you, Mrs. Bray. I'm afraid Mr. Bray's busy. We've got a traveller in. Would you like him to ring you back? You know," she ended archly, "how he hates to be disturbed."

This familiarity annoyed Alice. She wished that Charles would find an assistant who was a lady. Miss Hubback had a common accent and Alice was sensitive to accents.

She said coldly, "I'm in a hurry."

Miss Hubback was breezy. "Oh dear. I'd better get him then, hadn't I?"

There was a chink as she laid the telephone down. Alice could hear her humming softly as she left the tiny office. Then Charles's voice said, "Are they all right?"

"Of course they are, dear. They've just got off the bus."

"Good. I'm sorry if I worried you."

"That's all right, dear. But I'm late for my little tea-party now, so would you do a small errand for me? I ordered a lobster from Goring and I haven't had time to pick it up. Do you mind?"

"Of course not. Why lobster?"

"The Wallaces are coming to dinner. Now don't say this is the first you've heard of it because I told you last week." She put on a soft, coaxing voice. "And, sweetheart, I know they're not really your sort of people but they really are such an interesting creative couple. So do try and be nice to them, won't you?"

"I'll be polite, I hope."

"Of course you will. You always are, dear. But I want you to be more than polite, really friendly."

His voice was suddenly testy. "Wallace is in advertising, isn't he? What's creative about that?"

"He's a very clever artist, dear. And Erna Wallace is so clever with her hands. She makes pots. Really interesting, modern ones."

"Does she now? Well, well. . . ." He cleared his throat. "All right, dear. I'll come home with the lobster. Enjoy your tea."

She put the telephone down. There was a thumping noise on the floor above. The ceiling shuddered and, in the dining-room, the glasses on the sideboard danced against each other with a sound like little bells. Auntie was getting up after her rest. Her massive footsteps trod across the upstairs landing to the bathroom. It was like a mountain moving. She turned on the bath and began to sing in her strong, melodious voice, "When I survey, the Wondrous Cross." Mingling with the splashing water, her voice rose painfully to the high note beyond her range and sank, gladly, to a swelling contralto. "On which the Prince of Glo-ry di-ed."

"Stupid old fool," said Alice loudly. Auntie had been living at Peebles for over a year and Alice felt she would never become used to her presence. Since her arrival, a distinct musty smell had hung about the bedroom floor and the old woman made unpleasant noises in the bathroom. Although she was rich, she never offered to contribute towards the household expenses. Alice had, on several occasions, discussed the rising cost of living in her presence but she had not taken the hint. On the other hand, Charles was her favourite nephew. . . .

"Mummy," Hilary called. "Mummy." Her voice was high and eager. She ran in at the gate but when she saw her mother she stopped abruptly and stood uneasily still, rubbing one dusty sandal up and down the back of her leg. Her face took on an expression of dumb idiocy.

Alice knew that Hilary was pleased to see her and too shy to show it, nevertheless she was irritated, as always, by the child's inability to express an attractive emotion.

She said, "What a mess you're in. Surely you don't have to get so dirty?"

Hilary squirmed her shoulders and did not answer. Peregrine came up to Alice, carrying a pail full of shells.

"Look," he said, "I've got lots of pink ones. I'm going to make a necklace for your birthday."

There were dark rings of tiredness round his eyes. His cheeks were flushed with a pale, delicate colour.

"Are you, love?" Alice kissed him lightly on the top of his head. Feeling Hilary's smouldering eyes upon her, she said, "Did you collect any shells, darling?"

"Yes. I threw them away, though. Nasty, dirty things." Hilary exaggerated her disgust. "Dead fish's houses."

Janet said, "She emptied them all over the promenade. It was a filthy mess, all mixed up with sand and seaweed. And *I* had to clean it up." She looked hot and cross, her mouth was sullen. Alice felt annoyed: surely it wasn't too much for the girl to take the children out occasionally? She did nothing else except her silly, part-time job as secretary to the local dentist: she had no particular talents.

Alice said sweetly, "What a bore for you. You won't mind giving them their tea, will you? It's all ready. I expect Hilary will be a good girl and help, won't you, Hilary?"

Hilary scowled and squinted down her nose.

"For heaven's sake, child, take that look off your face."

Hilary gave her mother a bitter glance and hopped on one foot into the house, leaving a trail of damp sand behind her. Following, Peregrine carried his pail tenderly, like a chalice.

Janet said in a detached voice, "Hilary is much fonder of you than Peregrine is. You wouldn't think it, would you?"

Alice wondered if this was intended as a reproach (she knew she was often harsher with her daughter than with Peregrine because she loved her more) but decided at once that it was unlikely. Janet was much too anxious that Alice should approve of her to be critical: sometimes her evident devotion had touched Alice's intelligence though it never had, and never could, touch her heart. Still, the knowledge of it had softened her exchanges with her stepdaughter and made it easier for her to tolerate her stupidity and lack of grace. Lately, however, Alice had fancied that Janet's attitude towards her had curiously changed: her manner had become a good deal less humble, and, at the same time, almost excessively considerate. Occasionally she would fuss over Alice as if she were someone quite old and frail: with gentle autocracy she forbade her to sit in draughts. Alice had been amused, but only to a point. That point was reached on the day that she surprised a look of pity on the girl's face. She had told herself that it was inconceivable that Janet should be sorry for her. Nevertheless the fleeting expression had affected her like an insult. From that moment, a new tartness had crept into their relationship.

Now Janet said, "I'm sorry. That was a beastly thing to say to you." The clumsy apology implied condescension.

Alice said coldly, "Please do not trouble to explain my own child to me."

The unfairness of this remark worried her briefly after Janet had gone, silent and rebuked, into the house. Then she looked at her watch, saw that she was really very late, now, and went out to tea.

It was nearly closing-time. Charles brought in the trays of secondhand books from their position on the narrow pavement outside the shop. Turfed out from cobwebbed attics, novels, travel books, Christmas annuals, the sermons of forgotten Victorian vicars, jostled each other in their dusty jackets, offered for sale at sixpence each. He picked up a bound volume of *Chatterbox* and lingered over the lovingly tattered pages. There had been a copy, he remembered, in his preparatory school library—a dignified term for the rough rows of shelves in one corner of the room where they kept their play-boxes.

The shop bell tinkled and he thrust the *Chatterbox* on one side. Miss Hubback had come back with the lobster.

"Look, it's a beauty. Fresh caught this morning. Are you having a dinner party, Mr. Bray?"

The lobster, unwrapped from its newspaper, had a curiously exotic air.

Charles thought of Erna Wallace, a trivial, eager woman, twittering in endless, flowing scarves, trying hard to live up to Alice's idea of her as a contemporary potter.

"Well, yes . . . or rather, my wife is." He smiled. It was difficult not to smile at Miss Hubback. Although she was in her thirties, she was as clumsy and engaging as a very young girl. Her face was almost quite round and artless as a child's first drawing. Her features, which were small and elegant, rather like those of a china doll, seemed lost in the middle of it. Good will shone out of her like innocence in a tired world.

She said, "I think your wife is lovely, Mr. Bray."

"Oh?" Though used to her sudden, bursting confidences, Charles was surprised.

Her eyes glistened shyly behind her spectacles. "I shouldn't say that, should I? I mean it was sort of personal, wasn't it?"

"I've always found you can be as personal as you like, provided what you say is flattering."

She gave a high, neighing laugh, "Oh, Mr. Bray, you *are* cynical." She gazed at him admiringly. "Honestly, I wasn't being flattering. I know you'll laugh at me, but that evening I came to dinner was the most wonderful experience of my life."

"I wouldn't dream of laughing at you," he said, "what was so special about the party?"

She beamed. "It was all so lovely. The way your wife talked about important things, not just small talk. It was like being at a university. Your home is lovely, too. I thought the lounge was like something out of *House and Garden*."

"I'm glad you liked it." And he *was* glad, he told himself. But sorry, too, that she had been taken in by something so second hand.

He said, "We'd better lock up."

"Already? It isn't quite time. . . ." She looked at him doubtfully.

"It's all right. I'll do it. You run along home early for once."

As she fetched her coat, she said, "Isn't it dreadful? About the poor little girl?"

"What? Oh . . . yes."

45

"They were talking about it at the fishmonger's. I hope they catch him soon. Hanging's too good for a man like that," she ended savagely.

He was shocked. "Poor devil. I don't suppose he's responsible for his actions."

"You're sorry for *him*?" she cried. "But aren't you worried? I'm sure poor Mrs. Bray must be. Your lovely, lovely babies." Her tiny mouth quivered sentimentally.

He said, evading the issue, "My wife is very sensible. She doesn't worry unnecessarily."

When Miss Hubback had gone, clipping on her run-over heels along the cobbled passage that smelt of herring and salt to the broad, main street with its bright, light shops, Charles put up his green wooden shutters and locked the heavy iron bars into place.

The exertion made his head swim: he rested, leaning against the counter. Then the dizziness passed and he flexed his muscles cautiously, feeling for the pulse in his wrist with tender hypochondria. Reassured, he smiled. It was nothing. Nothing to worry about, the doctor had said, just a timely warning that he must take things easily. The plain truth was that we were none of us as young as we used to be. But with care, a monthly check-up, there was no reason why he should not make old bones. The old heart—the doctor spoke with a blunt, dismissing cheeriness—was a bit coked up like the cylinders of an old car engine. They had both smiled at the professional joke and, when the interview was over, shaken hands.

At first, Charles had been dismayed. Then, as the months passed and his condition grew no worse, he began to treat the doctor's diagnosis with light contempt. Talking with his friends, he frequently led the conversation round to the inefficiency of the medical profession. He was delighted whenever he discovered an instance when they had been proved wrong. He did not worry overmuch about himself. Nevertheless, he did not tell Alice about his monthly visits. He did not wish to spare her, but himself: once told, she would be brave on his behalf and insist that he face up to it. She was a very courageous woman.

In the middle of the night, Peregrine woke and screamed. Hilary got out of bed and went to him. His hands, clutching at her nightdress, were sticky and hot.

"It's all right," she crooned, "all right. Hilly's here."

Pushing her arm aside, he stared into her face with dark, glittering eyes, words stumbled out between great, hiccoughing sobs. "The Devil came and sat on the end of my bed. He was black. There were wings round his head."

Hilary looked round the nursery and saw the chipped, white-wood furniture, unearthly in the moonlight but unmistakeable. Their flannel dressing-gowns hung, grey and shapeless on the back of the door; their clothes, draped baggily over their separate chairs, were only clothes. The painted, gleaming eyes of the rocking-horse gave her a lurching moment of fear, but she spoke soothingly.

"There's nothing here. Only the toys and things and me. Go to sleep."

His eyelids drooped. She hugged him maternally and said, to comfort herself, now, "If there had been anyone here, I'd have seen him too."

She felt a shudder go through him. He stiffened and sat bolt upright, beating the bedclothes with clenched fists.

"He was here, he was. I didn't see him with my eyes. I saw him out of the back of my head. He was awful."

There was nothing to be said to *that*. She pressed him with delicious fearfulness but he either would not, or could not, answer. Nothing else that he said was at all lucid. The fearful vision was fading fast and there was nothing left but terror. When she tried to make him lie down he resisted her with wiry strength and cried for his mother.

She tried to comfort him. "It's all right now. If you like, you can come into my bed. If you promise not to wet it."

He fought her off frantically. "Mummy." His voice rose wildly. In moments of disaster, he always turned to his mother, believing that once he reached her, he would be safe. Hilary would have liked to think that this was true but knew it was not: this was the difference the years had made between them.

Peregrine got out of bed and hobbled across the linoleum, his pyjama trousers round his ankles, his small behind gleaming. Hilary got back into her own bed and tried to warm her feet by wrapping her nightgown round them.

She heard Peregrine's voice on the landing, outside their mother's door. It was raised in a loud, formless wail, a cry of lamentation. No words could be distinguished. A door opened and there was a rush of voices. Peregrine's cries died as he was carried into the room and the door was closed.

Hilary dozed, her head on the cold pillow. Distantly, she was aware that the whole household was awake. Someone had closed the nursery door but the landing light shone in a streak beneath it. She heard her father's voice, then Janet's.

A little later, the door opened and a shaft of light sprang across the room. Peregrine was carried in, limp in his mother's arms. His legs and arms dangled loosely, he made no sound. Alice's hair, out of its braid, hung gloriously to her waist. Lying on her side, Hilary watched her with one jealous eye, the other being pressed into the pillow.

Janet said, from the doorway, "Will he sleep now?"

Hilary could only see her by moving her eye so far round in its socket that it hurt.

Alice made a shushing sound. Then she bent over Peregrine, tucking him up. She turned towards Hilary's bed and Hilary closed her eyes tightly. She felt her mother's breath like a small cold wind on her skin, but the kiss she expected did not come.

Alice left, rustling, and Hilary heard her whispering on the landing. "*She's* asleep, anyway. Did you hear him, crying about the Devil?"

Janet muttered. Then she said more loudly, ". . . all Hilary's fault. I expect she was trying to frighten him."

"Why didn't you tell me?" said Alice, exasperated. Hilary raised her head from the pillow and listened. Grownup anger, except when it was directed against herself, excited her.

"It didn't seem important. I forgot about it. She said Peregrine had seen the Devil. I thought—some story of Nanny's. You know what *she* was."

"She's a naughty little girl." Their voices grew softer. They both laughed.

Then Janet said, gruffly, "You ought to go to bed. You'll catch cold."

The light was switched off. A little later the lavatory cistern flushed with a sound like baying wolves. A door closed and the house was silent.

Hilary lay in the dark and listened to the sea. It was loud and angry to-night. She pictured it, crawling up the crumbling cliffs and sweeping in through the doors and windows, drowning them all in their beds.

Peregrine was whimpering in his sleep, now and again he gave a short, yapping sound like a dreaming puppy. Hilary rolled on to her tummy and stuffed the edges of the pillow against her ears. Anger possessed her. Why should

49

she be blamed because Peregrine had seen the Devil? It was unfair. She squeezed out a few, hot tears and tasted them with her tongue. She would pay Peregrine out, she decided. To-morrow she would think of a way to punish him.

Chapter Three

In his caravan on Grey's Field, the man slept, fully clothed, beneath an army blanket. In his dream was a beautiful, laughing child. He loved her and stretched out his hands but her face twisted with ugly fear and she ran away. Then his mother was angry with him. He became frightened and restless and began to mutter in his sleep.

Towards morning, it grew perceptibly colder. He woke in his stinking bunk and said, "Chip-chop-change, weather gone, weather gone, chip-chop-change." At first he thought it was his mother speaking and then he knew it was not. She was dead and gone, dead and shut in a box. They had taken her away down the narrow stairs; the coffin had jammed in the turning and they had sweated in their black coats until, in the end, they had sawn away part of the banister rail. Four black horses with polished shoes and feathery plumes had drawn her carriage to the cemetery. All that she owned had been sold to pay for the funeral. When she was buried, his aunt had sat on the shiny, leather couch in the parlour and mourned: what shall we do now, what shall we do with the boy?

Grumbling and shivering, he sat on the edge of the bunk and felt beneath it for his surgical boot. When he found it, he dangled it limply between his knees and stared vacantly across the narrow limits of the caravan to the naked, grease-smeared wall. A low table, covered with cracked linoleum, stood between the bunk and the wall: on it lay a bar of

Nut Crunch and a blue saucer full of bird seed. In one corner of the caravan there was a Primus stove and a kettle, in another, a pile of empty bean-tins, old seed-cartons and mouldy hunks of bread. His housekeeping was methodical and simple. Every day he wiped the table with a wet cloth and swept the floor. Once a week, he shovelled the pile of rubbish into a sack and threw it into the sea at high tide. He never changed his clothes.

It came to him, dimly, that it was time for him to go, but he did not stir. Pearly-grey light came through a small window cut in the door. Hanging in front of it, was a bird cage covered with a torn piece of rag and now, as the man sat on the bunk, the canary began to twitter sleepily. With a grunt, the man heaved himself upright and fastened the boot on to his dreadful foot. Limping across the caravan, he removed the covering from the cage and said tenderly, "Woke up, have you, Johnny?" The bird ruffled its feathers and regarded him with eyes that were like small chips of black boot polish. It made no sound.

Chirruping gently, he filled his palm with seed and opened the cage door. The bird fluttered out, landed on his middle finger and began to peck at the seed. When it had finished, the man laughed and tossed the bird into the air. It flew round the caravan and settled on a ledge above the bunk, watching him while he lit the stove and put the kettle on. He made strong tea in a brown-ringed mug and drank it slowly; between sips, he chewed on a piece of bread that he had taken out of his pocket. Then he called the canary and it came to him. He held it in his hand, caressing its feathers and murmuring love words before he put it back in the cage.

He picked up the bar of Nut Crunch and stepped out into the cold air. The sun was just coming up. He went quickly across the field, between the sleeping caravans, until he reached a blue and white painted one that stood by the gate, its long shafts resting on the ground. A small tent was erected on its lee side, the thin canvas sides bulged with movement.

The man stopped and sucking his lower lip, whistled softly. The flap opened and a small, dark head appeared.

"It's all right, girlie," he said softly. "It's only Uncle. What do you think I've got for you?"

The gipsy eyes sparkled. "Lolly?"

"Something nicer than that. Will you give Uncle a kiss for it?"

The child pouted. "Dunno. What for, anyway?"

"Crunchie Bar," he said and held it up in front of her. Her face became pinched with greed, her tongue crept out between her kitten's teeth.

She taunted him. "My Dad says I'm not to speak to you. You're a loony. That's what my Dad says. All them that sweeps the roads, they're all loonies."

He crouched on his haunches and threw the Crunchie Bar on the ground between them. She stared at him suspiciously. Then she wriggled out of the tent on hands and knees. She wore a cotton vest and navy knickers, round her small neck hung a thin, gold chain with a dependent cross. The man had found it in the gutter a few days before and given it to her.

She made a sudden dive and kissed him damply and swiftly, her coarse, curly hair tickling his cheek. He tried to take her in his arms but she evaded him and fled back to the tent. He followed her. Lifting the flap, he peered inside. She was crouching at the far end on a safari bed.

"You forgot your Crunchie Bar," he said.

She shook her head. "Go away. Don't want your mouldy old Crunch Bar."

A dog barked in the field and he glanced swiftly over his

53

shoulder. A boy was standing by the steps of a caravan about thirty yards away and watching him.

The man dropped the flap of the tent and began to limp away towards the gate. The boy bent with a quick gesture and jerked his arm forward as if he were throwing a stone. The man ducked instinctively and quickened his pace. The boy laughed loudly and put his thumb to his nose.

Above, in the cold sky, there was a pale ring round the sun.

Hilary had been awake since six o'clock. Wearing her Dayella nightgown, frilled at the neck and wrists and covered with pink rosebuds, she stood on a cane-bottomed nursery chair, her nose pressed against the cold glass of a small aquarium. The water was the colour of weak tea, faintly cloudy as if a dash of milk had been added to it. Dark shapes moved mysteriously over the glass sides and clustered on a smooth, spotted stone.

There were no fish in the aquarium. Once, long ago, there had been two mountain minnows: they had died within a day of each other. Hilary had not mourned their death for they had been dull and disappointing fish, quite unlike the glorious, flashing creatures she had hoped for. The tank had been a birthday present and one that she had chosen; she had imagined a glittering, alien world like the tanks in the pet shop, with bright, fantastic shapes gliding between waving water-weed. When she saw the small tank and the drab minnows, she had wept. Alice had been understanding and reasonable. She said she understood Hilary's disappointment but she had expected too much. Tropical fish could only live in heated water and such a tank would have been too expensive a present, wouldn't it, for such a little girl?

Once the minnows were dead, however, Hilary had lost her desire for fish. There were snails in the tank and she

54

loved them dearly, feeding them, when she remembered, with dandelion leaves gathered from the garden. In the beginning, there had been only two snails but they had multiplied rapidly and incestuously: now there were so many that it was impossible to count them. The biggest were the size of her thumb nail and the smallest barely visible: minute dots crowding on the green stalk of the one, fragile weed.

Hilary talked to them in a maternal voice, calling them by name in the manner of Miss Spiegler checking the roll call at school. "Bernice, Chloe, Ariadne. . . ." Her lips moved against the glass, making a damp, cloudy pattern. To spite Peregrine, she had insisted that there were no boy snails in the aquarium.

When she heard the dust-cart, she jumped off the chair and went to the window. Lately, she had not bothered to look out at the sweeper in the mornings but to-day she was bored. Peregrine, who usually woke before she did, was still sleeping soundly, breathing heavily through his open mouth.

The nursery looked out over the road and the high window was barred with vertical, iron rods. Holding on to the bars, she climbed on to the sill and peered through them.

The man was two or three houses away, sweeping the gutter with a long, smooth movement and picking up the dirt with his spade. She could see the top of his head, covered with a tweed cap. As he came nearer, almost opposite the front gate of Peebles, she began to tap with her fingers on the window pane. This was a game the children had played the summer before: Hilary had forgotten it until this moment. You tapped on the window until the dustman or the postman looked up and then you hid behind the nursery curtains. If you attracted their attention without being seen, you won a point. If you were spotted, you lost two.

The man glanced up briefly and went back to his sweeping. He was a different man from the one she remembered from last summer's game and yet there was something familiar about him. Suddenly, for no reason at all, she was afraid. Fear twisted deliciously in her stomach. She dreaded the moment when he would look up again and yet she longed for him to see her. She banged her knuckles loudly on the window pane.

This time, he looked up at once. Leaning on his long broom, he scanned the windows of Peebles with flat, incurious eyes. His gaze was long and leisurely and rested, finally, on the nursery window. There was no perceptible change in his manner, no suggestion in the white, uplifted face that he saw anything unexpected or out of the ordinary but he remained, for an endless stretch of empty time, quite immobile and staring at the window.

She knew him now, for certain, and the knowledge was terrible. She pressed herself against the cold bars, hoping that stillness might save her. What she could not see from the window, her memory supplied: the wide, black coat sweeping low over the twisted foot. Feeling his eyes burn into her, she gave a low cry and closed her own. Holding herself rigid, she thought: he won't recognise me, not in my nightgown. And then she knew, with awful certainty, that God had marked her for just this occasion. For what other reason, when she had been born so plain, had she been given her one beauty, her bright, unmistakeable, red hair?

She did not see him go. When she opened her eyes, he was walking away, pushing his green cart. Her fingers hurt: she loosened them slowly from the bars and saw that they were covered with dark grains of rust. Peregrine was awake, he was watching her sleepily from the bed.

"It was *Him*," she said, jumping down from the sill and

running to him for comfort. She crouched, shivering, on his bed.

"Who?" he asked, yawning and stretching his legs beneath the bedclothes.

She remembered his recent betrayal of her and stiffened.

"I shan't tell you," she said heavily, getting off the bed and hauling her nightgown over her head. She stood naked, a paunchy child with a tendency to bandy legs and scratched her buttocks. She knew that in punishing him she was depriving herself of a certain comforter but she did not shrink from her decision.

"You're a traitor," she said. "In the Middle Ages, they used to burn traitors at the stake. You're bound," she ended with relish, "to come to a bad end."

The pallor of his cheeks, the mournful gaze of his dark eyes, produced a mounting excitement in her. She had an easily diverted temperament.

"It would be dreadful to burn," she went on. "Think how it hurts if you scald your finger under the hot tap. It would be a thousand, thousand times worse than that."

Meekly, he bowed his head in the face of her just anger.

"I didn't mean to," he protested in a weak and injured tone. He blinked rapidly at her and promised, "You can borrow my pen if you like."

She hesitated before this attractive offer. Then she said, "Don't want your beastly old pen. It writes like a spider walking." She hitched up her knickers and pulled on her gingham dress.

He looked at her plaintively. "I don't feel well," he prevaricated. "You'd be sorry if I died."

His lack of fight drove her to worse excesses. "I wouldn't be sorry. I'd dance and laugh. If you were burned, you'd smell like roasting meat." She rolled her eyes and smacked her lips appreciatively.

He snivelled sadly into the sleeve of his pyjamas and she regarded him contemptuously. "Cowardy custard," she said. She left the nursery and closed the door.

The landing glowed with a weird, green light. At Peebles, the windows on the staircase, in the lavatory and at the sides of the front door, were of stained glass. Alice, when she had re-decorated the house and hung prints from Picasso's blue period on the walls, had wanted to remove the coloured glass but on this point, Charles had made one of his rare, determined stands. As a child, he had thought the colours rather jolly and he was sentimental about his childhood. He knew the stained glass was old-fashioned but it still seemed to him a fairly pleasing folly and he could not understand why it should offend his wife. When friends came to the house Alice pretended that she thought the glass amusing.

Hilary looked at her pale green hands and felt like a rare, strange creature in the depths of the sea. As she went down the stairs, she saw the morning newspaper and the letters lying on the mat before the hall door, bathed in a soft, religious light. The segments of glass in the narrow window by the door were blue and yellow and rosy red.

She picked up the letters and examined them carefully. There were two for her father and several for Alice. These she dismissed: her parents' letters were seldom interesting. The remaining letter was for Janet and this she examined with care. The bulky envelope had been posted locally and the address was written in a fine, flowing hand.

"Prying little pig," said Janet, suddenly appearing behind her. She was dressed in dark-blue linen and the skin of her face was pale and slippery as if she had been crying.

Hilary was shocked by her sudden, stealthy appearance. Concealing Janet's letter in the pocket of her dress, she said accusingly, "I didn't hear you come down."

"I daresay you didn't. I was in the kitchen. I've been up for hours. Were you going to open the letters?"

Hilary answered truthfully, "I don't know." Janet picked up the letters and looked through them. The envelope was burning a hole in Hilary's pocket. She said rudely, making matters worse, "There wasn't one for you, anyway."

"I can see that." Janet laughed nervously and touched the white bow at her throat.

"I don't suppose Uncle Aubrey can be bothered to write to you every day," said Hilary outrageously. "I expect he thinks you're silly, really." She looked uncertainly at her half sister. "Soppy Janet," she said.

Janet did not answer. She did not even look angry. The expression of her eyes was sad and sorrowful; her dejected appearance depressed Hilary. Sighing gently, she stood on one leg and scratched the back of her knee with the toe of her sandal. She had not intended to steal the letter but she could not possibly replace it now without Janet noticing. The corners of her mouth turned downwards, she sighed again.

Janet was relieved, rather than upset, because the letter she expected had not come. Lately, Aubrey's long, poetic letters had begun to bore her. She was no longer impressed by his poetry—most of it, she considered, was too bad to be flattering to her and the good bits had a familiar ring. Her critical attitude distressed her although she was sure that her feelings for Aubrey were unchanged. She did not love him less because she could not bear to. It was so much more important to love than to be loved: if she should cease to love Aubrey, what would happen to her? Her heart would be empty, her life a desert. She had been thinking a good deal about the death of love in the past few weeks and had often wept in private.

She heard Hilary sigh and looked down on her with lofty pity. "Other people's letters are much duller than you think they're going to be," she said kindly. "Isn't it your turn to lay breakfast?"

"I suppose so," Hilary agreed, and went with leaden feet into the dining-room.

Scowling at the sunlight that lay in dusty shafts across the table, she slapped the place mats down on the dark, polished wood and set out the cutlery. She took the pepper and salt from the sideboard, the coloured tile for the coffee pot and the bottle of Worcester sauce for Auntie. The napkins, rolled in their rings of Italian straw, were jumbled among the knives and forks. Glancing over her shoulder, she took the letter out of her pocket, opened it, screwed up the pages to make it look like an old letter, and stuffed it at the back of the linen drawer. This action made her feel worse, not better. She frowned at her reflection in the silver sugar-basin. The curved sides widened her face into a fat, pale slab in which wicked, piggy eyes glinted angrily. She thought she had never seen anything so horrible, so empty of hope.

"Ugly beast," she addressed the face. "Horrible Hilary. Everyone hates you."

Depression dragged her down into the pit. She was unwanted, set apart from other people. She read letters that did not belong to her and, in her incurable greed, stole chocolate biscuits from the larder. She felt her badness grow inside her like a dark flower. She wanted to shout, to stamp her feet and cry. She heard her mother talking to Peregrine in a loving voice as she came down the stairs.

"Put on your blue jersey, darling, the weather's changed. Hurry, or we'll start breakfast without you."

Hilary pushed her porridge round her plate. She made a contour map with islands of porridge and rivers of milk.

"Don't mess your food about," her mother said. "Look how nicely Peregrine behaves."

Beside his sister, Peregrine ate daintily, his napkin tied round his neck. He hated to get his clothes dirty; if he were to drop porridge on his trousers they would have to be changed immediately. After his first, nervous glance at Hilary as he slid into his seat, he had been too embarrassed to look at her. He knew, though he had forgotten how or why, that he had let her down and the knowledge of his own inadequacy distressed him.

Opposite the children, Auntie mumbled at her food and read the *New Statesman*. Her mouth was pouchy and lined and soft, her whole face sagged in worn creases like an old leather handbag. White drifts of talcum powder lay on either side of her nose. She was grossly old: her eyebrows bristled like a man's and the hair on her head was so sparse that areas of skin, pink and soft as a baby's, showed through the thin, grey strands. She wore a shapeless dress of grey alpaca held at the waist by a linked, silver belt sent, long ago, from India by an elder, bachelor brother. A knitted cardigan of beige wool was fastened at her pulpy throat by a ruby and emerald brooch. Her chief and lasting impression was one of excellent quality as if she had been fashioned out of the best materials and built to last. In order to impress a world that no longer cared about her, she acted several, deliberate character parts. Sometimes she was the imperious, eccentric aristocrat, sometimes she infuriated Alice with a display of excessive humility. Beneath her various poses she concealed a shy defended heart. She loved Charles as tenderly as a very young girl: Alice, she thought, was nowhere good enough for him.

Now, she pushed a piece of bacon on to Charles's plate.

"I don't need it as much as you do. I'm only an old woman."

Alice put down the popular morning paper she was reading. "Auntie, there's enough for everyone," she said sharply.

The old woman ignored her. Alice sighed and, leaning across the table, passed the newspaper to her husband. She said something in French.

Hearing the unfamiliar language, Hilary looked up. Her parents were discussing something with their eyes: their faces were set and ominous. She said, to attract their attention to herself, "Can we go on the beach this morning?"

Meaning glances were exchanged. Alice answered her brightly. "Not this morning, dear. Janet can't take you."

"Why can't we? We sometimes go by ourselves," Peregrine said innocently. His blank, sweet gaze went from one parent to another. Sensing a mystery, a faint line showed between his brows.

"Just because, dear." She spoke carefully to Charles. "*Que pense-tu?* Unwise in the circumstances, don't you think?"

A heavy silence hung over the table. The children watched their parents uneasily. Janet and Auntie went on eating. Charles rose from the table and cleared his throat. He said uncomfortably, "Might be a good idea to keep them away from the holiday crowds just now."

Hilary said, "People are always going on holiday. I don't see why *we* can't have a holiday."

"But you live by the sea," chided her father, smiling.

"A person can get tired of the sea," Hilary said coldly.

Alice said indulgently, "If you're a good girl, we'll all go on a real holiday one day. We might even go abroad. That would be nice, wouldn't it?"

Charles, passing behind Hilary's chair, ruffled her burning hair. She twisted round and smiled up at him, her rare, refulgent smile.

"Can I come too?" asked Peregrine, interested.

"Of course, my darling." Alice beamed on him. "We'll all go. There is so much to see, you'll love all the funny foreign places." She caught her breath and looked at Charles. "Why not, after all? Spain is cheap just now. Charles, let's go to Spain."

"We could see a bull-fight," added Hilary happily.

Everyone smiled: a pleasant atmosphere of family concord filled the room.

Janet destroyed it. Her voice was thick and hoarse. "We could go to Paris, couldn't we? Paris is lovely, especially in the spring. The blossom is out along the Seine and you can sit at the little cafés and watch the people go by. That's what you said, isn't it? Only *I* never got there, did I?"

She flung the question at Alice with bitter, trembling intensity. It shocked them all. They sat silent and stared at her blazing eyes. Then Janet began to cry. "Always promises, promises. Why do you do it?" Leaving the room, she slammed the door.

"Well," said Charles. He raised his voice. "Janet, come back here at once."

"Leave her alone, dear." Alice was pale. "It's my fault. I said—oh, years ago—that we'd take her to Paris. It wasn't serious. Has she hated me for this, all this time?"

Hilary thought Janet was stupid. Why couldn't she see that it was only a game? And her mother was hurt. She looked beautiful and sad.

She said chivalrously, "Silly Janet. It's all right, Mummy. *She* doesn't understand when you're only pretending. She wants everything to be true, always."

Alice addressed her resentfully, as if she were an adult. "You saw that, did you? What a fool I am."

"My dear girl." Charles went to his wife and patted her shoulder. Peregrine began to cry silently. He was violently affected by family tension. The tears, like pale, transparent pearls, rolled down his cheeks and splashed on to his napkin.

"It's all right, old chap," his father said.

"Why can't we go on the beach?" Hilary demanded. "I want to go. We don't need Janet, we can play by ourselves. . . ."

"You can't go because I say you can't," cried Alice hysterically. "Must you go on and on?"

Auntie got up from the table. "Have you finished with the newspaper?" she asked. She was quite unaware of what had been happening. "I'll leave you the *Statesman*. Excellent article by Crossman. . . ."

She felt for the silver-mounted stick which she felt suitable to her age and monstrous size and leaned on it heavily. She did not need it, being as strong as a horse and capable, still, of a ten-mile walk. Looking at the paper in her hand, "I see they've found that poor child," she said.

Alice and Mrs. Peacock were in the kitchen, washing up. They were talking in lowered voices. Hilary swung on the handle of the kitchen door, trying to hear what they were saying.

"I've had to bring my Wally. I couldn't leave 'im at home. Not after what's happened."

Seeing Hilary, Alice gave Mrs. Peacock a significant glance.

"Listeners hear no good of themselves," said Mrs. Peacock. She was a tiny woman with a skinny body of a little girl and a soft, savage face like a baby owl's. She had borne five sons and buried two husbands: it was somehow difficult to see her virginal body in connection with such a cavalcade of birth and death.

"Run along now," said Alice and Hilary went reluctantly into the garden.

Deep in the long grass, Wally was shooting at birds with a home-made catapult. He was a fat, pale boy, already a head taller than his mother. He had bad teeth and was very clever. He had just won a county scholarship to the local boy's public school.

"Can I have a go?" Hilary looked longingly at the catapult.

He shook his head silently and took careful aim. A small stone cracked through the branches of the chestnut tree.

"Please, Wally."

He ignored her.

"I've seen the Devil," she announced importantly.

He stared at her. "Liar. There ain't no such person."

"You shouldn't say 'ain't'. Liar yourself."

Wally walked, whistling, to the bottom of the garden and she followed him, trailing through the wet grass. She loved Wally deeply. He stopped suddenly and she bumped into him, treading on his heels.

He gave a squeal of pain. He detested being hurt. "Mess off, can't you?" he said furiously. She fled tearfully towards the house and he called after her, "Fatty. Fatty lump."

Hilary closed the door of Auntie's room softly. She had never been forbidden the room but she knew that if her mother knew she was there, she would be sent on an errand or told to play with Peregrine.

Leaning against the door, she breathed in the smell of the room, a smell compounded of old age and stiff, heavy clothes; the mustiness of blankets and rag rugs; a whiff of sweet, escaping gas from the popping fire. Then she threaded her way cautiously through the crowded furniture to the desk in the window. "Auntie," she said, and touched her on the arm.

"It's you, is it?" The old woman looked up from her letter. "Don't bother me now, I'm busy."

Hilary wandered round the room, picking up books and back numbers of periodicals. The room was small and stuffy, darkened by an elm tree outside the window. A heavy clock under a glass dome ticked the time away, its round, brass weight circling slowly. Hilary could remember the room before Auntie came, when it had been her father's study. His desk had stood under the window and his school pictures had hung on the walls. Alice had cleared it out angrily, saying, "It's good enough for *her*, isn't it? Or do you think my lady should have the best bedroom?"

Hilary found the morning newspaper crumpled on the sagging seat of Auntie's wing-chair. She lay on her stomach on the floor, dug her toes in the rag rug and spread the sheet out before her.

Poppet's picture was in the middle of the front page and Hilary looked at it with interest. She knew it was Poppet although her hair looked darker because of the bad printing of the photograph and the name underneath was different. She read the first few lines beneath the picture and a dark veil came down over her eyes. Her heart beat wildly in her throat. Something cold and evil menaced her from the shadowed corners and for a little while she crouched quite still, as if afraid to wake a sleeping beast.

Then she whispered, "Auntie." The erect, broad back did not move, the pen scratched unhesitatingly across the paper, but Hilary knew that she listened. She did not believe in Auntie's deafness. Auntie said that she heard and Hilary believed her. Comforted by the mountainous, calm presence, she went on in a louder voice, "I saw a man take Poppet away. She was on the beach with her mother and he came and took her. He told her he was going to take her to the Fun Fair. I expect he said something like that, don't you think? But he didn't take her to the Fun Fair. Peregrine said

66

he was the Devil. Do you think he was the Devil, Auntie?
She must have been a very naughty little girl."

Suddenly a new and closer fear assailed her. "Auntie, he
knows where I live. Will he fetch me away too?"

In the silence, her head sang with light, tripping voices.
Who will they send to fetch her away, fetch her away, fetch
her away? Choking, she scrambled up from the rug and ran
to the desk, looking up urgently into the leathery face. "Will
he come for me, too?"

Auntie felt the plucking fingers and looked at the moving,
anxious mouth. "Come for you? Who, dear?"

"The man in the newspaper."

"You naughty child. . . ." Auntie brushed her away
and, rising from her desk, lumbered across the room. Bending
stiffly, she screwed the page of the newspaper between her
hands, stuffed them in the wastepaper basket and kicked it
out of sight. She lowered herself into the wing-chair, breathing heavily.

"You're not supposed to read the newspaper. It's not
suitable. Your mother will be very angry." Her massive
shoulders hunched, her face became, suddenly, sad and
crumpled and very old. "I should never have let you see
it," she said.

Hilary saw, with astonishment, that Auntie did not care
about her. She was only concerned that her own carelessness
in leaving the paper lying about should not be discovered.
Uncertainly she promised, "I won't tell Mummy."

"No." Half to herself, Auntie mumbled, "She wants
to get me out of the house. All she needs is an excuse like
this. Charles wouldn't be able to stand up for me. He's a
good man, but just. He'd know I was in the wrong. And
what would happen to me? I'm old, my friends are dead.
I ask you, what would happen to me?"

The question escaped her lips in a little, whimpering

breath. Her trembling hands played with the brooch at her throat. Between the thick, blue veins, the flesh was livid white.

"Stop it," cried Hilary, terrified, "Oh, stop it."

Auntie's eyes flickered over her without awareness. In a little while she would, if she remembered, be ashamed of behaving like this before the child. Just now, she was absorbed in her spirit's cowardice and her body's failure. She dreaded Alice's anger. When you were old, nothing mattered except your physical comfort and security: without it, all her pretensions and eccentricities would wither, she would be a shell of an old woman. Her eyes watered with self-pity. "I'm old," she mourned, "old."

The door of the hot little room opened, letting in a cold blast of air. Janet stood there, one hand on the door jamb, her skirts swaying about her. She looked sullen, her hair was blown spikily about her face as if she had been running in the wind.

Seeing Hilary, she frowned. "You shouldn't be here, bothering Auntie." She ignored Hilary's tears, assuming that the child had broken something. The room was full of small china treasures and Hilary was clumsy. "Run along to the nursery," she said.

Moving her lips carefully, Janet asked, "Was she being a nuisance?"

"A nuisance? No, she is never a nuisance." Auntie sat upright in her chair. Without much effort, she drew her character round her like a sumptuous cloak, concealing the tell-tale rags of her reality. "There was nothing wrong with the child."

She spoke quite sincerely. She had already forgotten the cause of Hilary's tears. She was not deliberately self-deceptive, only very old and unwilling to remember her moments of weakness. Now she was herself again, as proud and unflinching as a stage dowager.

She said maliciously, "*You* don't like the child, of course. You've always been jealous of her. When she was a baby they were afraid to leave you alone with her in case you did her a mischief."

Janet peered at herself in the looking-glass and pulled her hair tightly away from her face. She observed the effect despondently. Turning towards Auntie, she mouthed, "I was rude at breakfast. *She* hasn't said anything yet, but she will. She's never liked me."

"Why should she?" said Auntie in a bracing voice. "When she married Charles, you were a very cross-grained little creature. You adored her and that irritated—no one could have stood it. You followed her round like a spaniel, brimming over with sad, suffering love."

"I only wanted her to love me," said Janet miserably.

"Don't brood over your misfortunes." Auntie was never happier than when giving advice. "You don't have to stay here. You're young, you could get away."

"What could I do?" she asked inertly. "What have I got to offer?" She looked at her disconsolate face in the glass and smiled experimentally.

"You're pretty enough."

"But when it's all I've got, it's not much, is it?"

"Looks aren't the only thing."

"I haven't anything else. All I'm fit for is to go clickety-clack, clickety-clack, typing in an office, giggling with the other girls. I'm not clever. I take after my mother."

Auntie shook her head. "I mean, if you want to get married, your looks will do. You have other assets—a compliant nature, for example—and you are very ready to admire. These things count for a lot. In the end, more than beauty. *I* was beautiful."

69

Taken aback by this cold calculation of her prospects, Janet gave her an incredulous glance. "Is it so important, then, to catch a man?"

Auntie looked at her. "I think so, yes. Once you've done it, you may wonder what all the fuss was about, but if you never do, you'll feel, all your life, that you've missed the most important thing. Of course, you can fill up your life with other things but they don't last and when you're old no one will know that you were pretty or clever. . . ." Her voice fading, she gazed out of the window at the elm tree. Janet fidgeted. After a moment or two the old woman dismissed her solitary thoughts and continued, "And it would be no good your taking a lover. It's marriage that is the badge of success. Once you've been married, everyone will know you've been loved."

The room was silent. Auntie brooded in her chair. On the point of departure, Janet drooped with inanition, stifling a yawn.

There was a scuffle on the landing. Immediately following her peremptory knock, Mrs. Peacock appeared on the threshold of the room. In spite of her frail, shrinking appearance, she had a large, dramatic soul: she made her entrance as to a roll of drums. For a long, impressive moment she waited, gathering their startled eyes.

Then she spoke. "Look at him. Just look at 'im."

Pulling the child forward into the room, she pointed to his face with her free hand. Peregrine, who could not bear her proximity, shrank away, his arms stretched to the limit. He was tear-stained and paler than usual. His upper lip was disfigured by a dark, spreading burn.

To their shocked cries, Mrs. Peacock returned a nod of grim satisfaction. "What a thing for a sister to do! She can't deny it. I caught her in the act. Holding his little mouth on to the bulb of her electric lamp. He'll be marked for life." She drew in her breath with a sharp, indignant hiss: the air quivered.

"The little beast," cried Janet. Falling to her knees, she gathered Peregrine into her arms.

"I told her straight. You're a wicked girl, I said, a wicked girl and God will punish you for this. She knew what she'd done *then*, I can tell you. . . ."

Groping for her stick, Auntie rose ponderously to her feet. "You had no right to say that. No right at all. You exceeded your authority. Where is she now?"

Mrs. Peacock did not answer. Before this frontal attack, her righteous indignation faded: an alarmed and sheepish expression crossed her face.

"Where is she?" Auntie insisted, thumping her stick on the floor, "What has become of the child?"

Chapter Four

In the playground of the Primary School, the children chattered like starlings. Their feet dragged and scraped on the grey asphalt. It was the first day of term and they were still drunk with the summer's freedom: their shouting and laughter rose to the blue roof of the sky. Presently, the cold clanging of the bell sobered them a little and they straggled out of the sunlight into the dark, stone doorway. Through the open window thumped the first, stolid bars of the morning hymn.

Beyond the high, fearsomely spiked railings, the body-guard of mothers lingered, their perambulators spilling out into the road. Toddlers, wailing at the inactivity, were slapped and given sweets to suck. On the opposite pavement, a young bobby in blue paced his beat self-consciously, his heart brimming over. A deeply sentimental man, he had been painfully affected by the death of poor Camelia Perkins and, seeing the waiting women, he loved them for the suffering which he was sure they must endure while her murderer was still at large in the town. He trod the ground with a heavy, solemn tread as if to tell them by his bearing that their children were safe with him.

At last the women began to disperse. Hilary, coming upon a group of them as she rounded a corner, dodged between the perambulators and ran on. They looked after her with a faint censorious interest. Why wasn't she at school? Perhaps she went to one of the private schools where term had not yet begun. You wouldn't believe, would you, that any mother would allow her little girl out alone at a time like this? In all their minds dawned the mild, unadmitted hope that if anything *were* to happen, they would have a chance to say that they had seen her. You couldn't mistake that hair. It was a lovely colour and, really, quite uncommon.

Hilary felt as exposed and helpless as a shelled crab. She was quite sure that her wickedness was already generally known. She was young enough, still, to believe that grown-up power was limitless: the long arm of authority could reach you anywhere. She saw the policeman out of the corner of her eye and thrust her head forward and down, hiding her face. It would not have surprised her if he had barred her way and accused her of murdering her little brother. Mrs. Peacock could easily have proclaimed her deed from the housetops and roused the town against her.

Her first tears had dried but she still wept inwardly. She felt no specific remorse, she wept out of a black and dreadful conviction that there was no hope for her. Burning with shame, she kept her eyes on the ground. Her whole being was concentrated in her plump knees and her squat feet in their flapping sandals. There was a long scratch on her left knee that she had not noticed until now. It puckered as she ran. This blemish became so vividly stamped on her memory that in later years she could never see a similar scratch on a child's knee without an associated feeling of guilt and misery.

She ran aimlessly, doubling back on her tracks and coming out finally upon the Downs, midway between Peebles and the town. There, she stopped running and trod the cropped turf gently, grateful for the cold wind on her hot cheek. A steep flight of wooden stairs, known to the children as the Hundred Steps, led from the cliff-top to the beach. As she went down them, the sea looked navy blue and still and the sun was stationary in the sky. At this end of Henstable, the promenade petered out into a narrow spit of concrete. There were no shops or stalls, no boats for hire. The beach was muddy and inclined to smell. The defences put up during the war had not been completely removed: here and there, gaunt iron structures remained. The disadvantages of this part of the shore gave it privacy and the trippers seldom visited it. The sober line of bathing-huts, shuttered now against the autumn gales, were rented only by the residents. Hilary wandered sadly among them, listening to the ebbing sea. It sucked back on the pebbles with a prolonged and musical roar.

She picked up a chalky stone and printed her name, in capitals, on the side of a hut. Then she drew a picture of Jesus on the Cross. As she worked over her drawing, including considerable macabre detail, she was filled with great unhappiness. *She* was innocent as *He* had been, as despised and rejected. The world was unjust and cold. A slow, sorrowful tear trickled from her eye.

She had not meant to hurt Peregrine. The whole thing had been his idea, not hers.

When she found him in the nursery he had been standing by her bed with the lamp already in his hand. Seeing the bulb glowing feebly in the strong daylight, she had reproached him.

"Look at you now, wasting electricity. Daddy will be angry."

(Charles was finicky about small economies. He would patrol the house after dark, turning off what he considered to be unnecessary lights. On the other hand, the extravagant

74

use of gas did not bother him: in winter, gas fires burned wastefully in almost every room.)

Ignoring what was, at Peebles, a commonplace remark, Peregrine looked at his sister with an exultant expression on his face and said that he was punishing himself. "For letting you down," he explained. He was a pupil at a day preparatory school where to stick up for the side was considered the whole duty of man. "I was holding it against my face and letting it burn me," he continued virtuously. There was no mark on his face.

For a moment, Hilary was at a loss. His triumph over her was complete: she felt small and shabby and mean. Then something, a kind of smugness in his attitude, a curious, suggestive brilliance in his eyes, made her realise that he knew quite well what effect his martyrdom would have on her. This was not real repentance. She became enraged.

"You haven't hurt yourself at all," she taunted him. "If you had, it would show."

His face fell. She had misjudged him partly: he had genuinely intended to burn himself and had, in fact, held the bulb against his face for some considerable time. That it had not, as yet, been hot enough to burn him, was scarcely his fault.

Hilary tossed her head. "It can't have hotted up properly. I bet it has by now."

Mournfully eyeing the lighted lamp, Peregrine feared that she was right. He hung his head. "Perhaps my skin doesn't burn easily. Not to show, I mean. I could have extra tough skin, couldn't I?"

He looked at Hilary pitifully, daring to hope that she would excuse him on these grounds. She frowned at him. The feebleness of his suggestion merely exacerbated his offence—how *like* him to try and wriggle out of it like that! Anger uplifted her: she did not count the cost.

"We'll see about that," she said in dark, meaningful tones that echoed the departed Nanny. "Come here this minute."

Completely in her thrall, he came, his eyes sad and mute. She took the lamp from him and held the bulb against his mouth. He was small and thin for his age and the littleness of his body, pressed against hers, the slight trembling that possessed him, gave her a wild and savage pleasure. She could have smashed his face, broken his bones.

Convinced that the punishment was just, Peregrine endured the pain for a full minute before he whimpered. Hilary took the lamp away and saw, appalled, the crimson mark on his upper lip. Her anger vanished and she was terrified. Everyone would see what she had done.

"Will it go away?" She begged, "Wash it and see."

Dutifully, he spat on his handkerchief and rubbed tentatively at the mark but it was too painful, his eyes filled with tears. He looked at himself in the mirror. "I look awful," he complained sadly. He was really upset by his appearance; he was a vain child.

Partly to console him but mainly because she hoped to stave off retribution, Hilary pressed the burning bulb against her own arm. If they saw that she too was hurt, surely they would not punish her? Looked at in that light, the pain, which was worse than she had imagined, was also welcome. She showed the mark to Peregrine. "Look. I've done it too. We can tell them we were playing a game, can't we? Spartans, or something like that." She remembered a story of which Peregrine was most curiously fond. "You know, like the brave little boy who let the wolf eat at his tummy."

"Why?"

"All right, don't," said Hilary, turning away. Her voice was muffled. "You don't love me very much, do you?"

Her bowed shoulders expressed utter dejection. Peregrine moved round so that he could see her face which was screwed up and plainer than usual. He was sorry for her because she was ugly. He thought, with a sudden flash of insight, that perhaps that was why she was so often naughty.

"You can tell them if you like, and I won't say it isn't true," he compromised. He was a truthful child but limited, more concerned with the letter than the spirit. At the moment, he was not particularly interested in justice. His mouth was hurting him and he did not really care what was said to the grown-ups one way or the other, although he knew that if Hilary were punished for burning him, it would only make more trouble for him later on.

But there was no opportunity for pretence. Mrs. Peacock came in just then and took in the situation at a glance. She ignored Hilary's explanation: she had had children of her own and knew a cook-up story when she heard one. She turned on Hilary indignantly. Her histrionic words, adding to Hilary's already violent sense of guilt, were too much for the child and she fled, weeping.

Now, re-living the episode, Hilary was seized with painful embarrassment. She could never go home, never, never. She flung the chalk stone away and ran to the farthest limit of the promenade. There were no steps down to the beach: the concrete simply came to an end in an abrupt and arbitrary fashion as if the builders had unexpectedly run out of materials or, suddenly, lost heart. She jumped down and continued along the deserted shore below the breakwaters at the edge of the tide. Here, the shingle ended in a desolation of sandy mud that sucked at her sandals. The beach was empty, the only sign of life far out at sea where the gulls fluttered like pieces of paper in the wake of a slow steamer.

The clay cliffs were high and bare with a narrow frill of grass on the top like green icing on a chocolate cake. The lower slopes were gentle but the children were forbidden to climb them because they were treacherous: from time to time, great slabs tumbled into the greedy sea. The erosion was not as rapid as on the marshy flats at the other end of the town but more dramatic: during a wild night in the previous winter, the entire garden of a house on the cliff top had slid neatly two hundred feet into a hollow where the banked flag irises continued to flower in season and a fishing gnome sat snugly by an ornamental pond.

Aware of the danger, Hilary climbed the cliffs. She hoped that they would fall on her. Death was preferable to the situation in which she found herself. Once she was dead, they would remember her with more love than they had shown to her in life. After a while, these mournful thoughts left her and she began to enjoy her freedom. She became a gallant explorer, opening up a waste land.

When she came, by accident, upon the fallen garden, she was elated. Earlier in the year, she had been taken to look at it from a safe distance on the cliff top. (Its comical preservation had become, this summer, a tourist attraction. The enterprising council had put up notices directing visitors to the spot from which it could most effectively be observed.) Hilary was not at all disappointed to find that the garden looked less perfect close to. She was only sorry because it seemed so neglected. The stone pond was cracked across the bottom and very dirty. She cleaned it up as well as she could with her handkerchief and tried to mend it with lumps of sticky clay. When this was done, she began to fill it with rainwater which she collected in a battered can from a depression in the cliff. It was laborious work but she became completely absorbed in it as the sun moved slowly across the sky.

Two elderly gentlewomen, pausing in their midday constitutional, saw her from the top of the cliff. One of them was rich and not quite right in the head, the other was paid to look after her. The companion, perturbed by the obvious danger of the child's position, urged that something should be done, but her employer, who had often been incommoded by the younger woman's attempts to rescue kittens from trees and stray dogs from teasing children, refused to discuss the matter. When she chose, she could be as deaf as a stone carving and, indeed, looked rather like one for she was aristocratic and so old that her flesh appeared to be made of some pale and indestructible material. After a while, the companion gave up trying and resigned herself to the conclusion that if they *were* to find someone to rescue the child, her parents, who were probably happily watching from some unseen vantage point, would accuse them of being a couple of interfering old spinsters.

"As of course, we are." The carving came to life suddenly and the companion was seized with a dreadful fear that, in addition to her other eccentricities, her charge had suddenly become able to read what went on inside other people's heads.

"A couple of nasty old maids. Stale virgins, good for nothing, barren as rock," went on the madwoman viciously. She was aware, in her saner moments, of her dependence upon this other woman whom she hated and despised and took great pleasure in embarrassing her. She went on to express the hope that the child on the cliff would be killed by a land-slide and so be saved from old age and suffering. She showed every sign of working herself up into one of her "states", but, having delivered herself of this outburst, she allowed herself to be appeased by the promise of a nice afternoon watching television and went home to lunch like a lamb.

By the early afternoon, Hilary had lost interest in the garden. She was hungry. She began to climb upwards. It was harder going than it had been on the lower slopes because the cliff top overhung in places. Once or twice, she was badly frightened by a slipping stone. She was not an agile child and she looked, from a distance, a very small and precariously balanced creature whose bright hair, when the sun caught it, flamed like a beacon against the brown mud of the cliff.

Auntie saw her from the shore.

The fuss and the flurry attendant on the child's disappearance had disgusted her. Her deafness saved her from the worst of it but even she could not escape the atmosphere at lunch-time. Tinned soup and bread and cheese were served to the family by Mrs. Peacock whose eyes were red and whose quivering sighs reminded them continually of the drama they were engaged in. The air trembled with hysteria. Auntie, pecking at her food, found it degrading.

After she had eaten, she went out. Leaving the house, she presented a dignified, if eccentric figure. Unlike most of the old ladies of Henstable, she wore no hat and her thin, grey hair streamed in the wind. She was wrapped in a dark blue coat made for her by a naval tailor, fastened at the throat with onyx buttons and lined with scarlet silk.

Like Hilary, she descended the Hundred Steps. She carried her stick, but made no use of it. Her walk was unfaltering, her head held high. At the end of the promenade, she climbed heavily down on to the shingle and walked along the beach, breathing a little faster than usual and with a bright look of pleasure in her eyes. After a short while she stopped and looked sharply round her. Seeing the empty beach, she removed her cloak and laid it, carefully folded, upon a flat stone. She slipped off her skirt and appeared clad below the waist in a capacious pair of waterproof bloomers. She took off her shoes and stockings and walked to the edge of the sea. She waded along the shore, her eyes fixed on the sucking water. Occasionally she bent and picked up a handful of sand, trickling it through her fingers. She prodded with her stick at drifts of seaweed, examining them closely. Finding an old, canvas shoe, she removed the sodden lace and tucked it into a specially made pocket in the front of her bloomers. Her face relaxed into lines of complete contentment.

Throughout the last year, she had gone beachcombing on every possible occasion. One October afternoon, shortly after she had come to Henstable, she had seen a set of false teeth floating on the scummy tide. She had kilted up her skirts and waded into the cold water, a curious excitement mounting within her. From that moment her afternoon walks had led her, almost as if some power outside herself had willed it, to the edge of the sea.

In the beginning, she looked only for things of value: wedding rings, silver coins, conch shells that she could sell to the flower shops as rose holders. But as her mania grew, she dropped all pretence of financial gain. She collected anything and everything; broken crockery, sodden garments, the bodies of dead gulls soaked in oil. She took home what she could and hid it secretly in her room. She found it increasingly difficult to reject things that could not be concealed at home: finally she found an empty petrol drum in a cave and there she stored the things that would decay and betray her. As her treasures became more important to her, she grew cunning. She had keys made for her drawers and bought an old wooden playbox with a padlock. She locked up carefully when she left her room. She trusted nobody.

This afternoon, she was unlucky. After the tennis shoe, she found nothing except a child's toy boat, its sails draggled by the sea. She disentangled the seaweed from the tiny mast and held it tenderly between her hands. She had fleeting thoughts of painting it blue and scarlet and mending the little sails but she knew she would not do this. She never mended anything.

She glanced casually up at the cliff. Although she knew she could be seen from the top of the cliffs, their high, sloping angle meant that the details of her activity were safe from prying eyes. Seen from that distance, she would look like someone shrimping.

She recognised Hilary reluctantly. For a desperate moment she pretended to herself that it might be any child. There were plenty of children with red hair. Then she saw her duty and feared it.

She must call out to the child, order her down to the beach and take her home. But she would have no time to dress: by the time she reached her clothes, Hilary would be out of sight. The child would have to see her as she was and her long, happy afternoons would be over. She saw her cherished occupation through unfriendly eyes as ludicrous and shameful: she saw, as vividly as if she stood before her, Alice's disgusted face. Her treasures would be torn from her, thrown disregarded into the dustbin. Henceforth, she would be watched continually, spied upon. They might even suggest that she was mad and have her put away.

At this thought, Auntie's face folded like a baby's. She began to whimper softly. Knee-deep in water, she shivered, hugging the toy boat to her breast. Up on the cliff, the child slipped and a stone rolled. Auntie hid her eyes with one, wet hand. Then, her face averted, she left the sea and ran heavily on her old, veined feet towards her clothes. She scrambled into them, her harsh breathing sounding like a wind instrument. The beach watched her with a thousand glittering eyes; the wide, empty silence mocked her cruelly. Panting, she fastened her cloak at her throat and made for the Hundred Steps. Their steepness almost defeated her. Half-way up she was forced to rest, clinging like a cripple to the slender rail. At the top she was too exhausted to carry out her intention of looking for Hilary: unusually bent, and leaning on her stick, she walked in at the gate of Peebles.

Alice, standing with her back to the drawing-room window, was visible from the garden path. As Auntie approached the front door, Alice flung out one hand in an emphatic, accusing gesture as if she were engaged upon a violent argument with someone in the room.

Auntie was relieved to see her. She had been afraid that Alice would be out, searching for Hilary. Now, she could tell her where to find the child. She had nothing with which to reproach herself: it had all turned out for the best. She had acted as promptly as she could and in the only possible way. She could not have climbed after Hilary. Even if she had been nimble enough, she was too heavy for those crumbling cliffs. And if she had shouted, Hilary would not have heard her: her old, thin voice would have been blown to silence by the wind. Much better to have done as she did, to have dressed quickly and hurried home for help. Convinced and comforted, she entered the house and pushed open the drawing-room door.

Janet, seated before the empty fireplace, was in tears. Alice remained where Auntie had seen her, at the window.

Her face was scarlet and her hair disarranged. Unable to hear, Auntie sensed her anger, a solid force barring her from the room. Like an actress in a silent film, Alice mouthed, gesticulated: Auntie shrank back before the violence of feeling that came from her.

She closed the door softly and retreated up the stairs. She could not face a scene, she was too old, too tired. Besides there was no need. Hilary was certainly on her way home. Why otherwise, should she have climbed the cliff?

By the time she was safe in her own room, Auntie was convinced there was nothing further that she could have done.

The cliffs stretched for five miles between Henstable and the next town along the coast. They were not part of Henstable like the Downs which were maintained at the ratepayer's expense and they had a bleak, forsaken look. They were, however, a favourite walk with the stouter of the town's ageing population and during the thirties, a dying and prosperous fishmonger who had quarrelled with his wife and saw no reason why she should live, after his death, in a manner to which his disposition did not entitle her, had provided the money for the building of five shelters on the cliff, one at each milestone.

When Hilary reached the top of the cliff, she went into the seaward side of one of these shelters and saw, through the glass partition, a middle-aged couple eating a sandwich lunch on the other side.

Her hunger became intolerable. She walked round the shelter and confronted the couple. "Could I have something to eat?" she asked. "I'm hungry."

They stared at her with bulging, unbelieving eyes. The man's face grew very red and his neck seemed to swell above his coat collar.

"Whatever next," he shouted. "Whatever next? Damned impertinence." Little specks of foam appeared on his lips. "Get along with you," he commanded in a strangled, military voice, "or I'll call the police."

Shame immobilised her. She stared with wide eyes, expecting him to rise from his seat and strike her. Then she turned and stumbled away. His voice pursued her, borne by the wind.

"You can say what you like, Myrtle. It's none of our business, none of our business at all."

Hilary ran inland, away from that terrible voice, into the fields where the sharp, wheat stubble pricked at her ankles and drew blood.

At the beginning of the second field, beyond the ditch, she came to the pipes. The pipes were a relict of a building project that had been abandoned when it became clear that this part of the cliff was being slowly swallowed by the sea. They were about fifteen feet long and made of cast iron. There was a large, official notice saying that anyone who removed or tampered with them would be prosecuted by Order.

She began to jump up and down on the pipes, singing in a loud defiant voice. Once or twice, she laughed out loud in an affected manner to show the man in the shelter that she didn't care. Then she forgot about him and decided to crawl through a pipe. This was an exciting and dangerous business because once you were properly inside a pipe, there was no retreat. It was impossible to turn round and difficult to go backwards. She selected her pipe and wriggled into it head foremost. The metal was cold against her skin and smelt of damp and rust.

She was half-way along when the circle of light at the end was blotted out. She lay, trembling and shaking, in utter darkness. Then, perhaps because her fear was too great to be borne, she accepted her destiny. On her elbows and knees, she moved forward into darkness.

When the light returned as suddenly as it had vanished, her faith was vindicated. She wriggled to the end of the pipe and poked out her head. The whiteness of the sunlight made her blink and it was some seconds before she saw, about two feet away from her and on a level with her eyes, the skirt of a black coat and a heavy, misshapen boot.

She remained quite still, her hands gripping the cold edge of the pipe. She was not surprised. She even gave a small nod of satisfaction as if to say: this is what I expected, after all. She had already met Him twice. If He were really the Devil, they had not been chance encounters. They had been written in her stars. A spring of gladness rose within her. There was no more need to be afraid. Confidently, she raised her eyes and smiled in welcome.

"To think that this should happen, to-day of all days," said Alice. "As if we hadn't enough to worry about." She added, sweepingly, "How *typical* of you."

It was hardly fair. Janet smarted beneath the injustice of it.

"It's *my* letter. You had no right to read it."

Her shocked voice reduced a principle to a smug, school-girl standard of values that was easy to dismiss.

"No *right*?" Alice was trembling from head to foot.

She had had a difficult day and was spoiling for a row. Her own fears for Hilary's safety had, initially, been diminished by Mrs. Peacock's prophecies of doom. These had grown momently more theatrical: listening to her, Alice had been forced into a position of unnatural calm. There was no real need to worry. It was absurd to make a fuss, impossible to see Hilary as a tragic victim. The child liked to be the centre of attention: she was bound to return, in search of an audience, if for no other reason, as soon as her temper had subsided.

By lunch-time, however, when there was still no sign of her, Alice was forced to admit that the matter was more serious than she had allowed herself to believe. Nagged by a feeling of guilt, she telephoned Charles.

He asked her when Hilary had gone out and when she told him, said, "You've left it long enough, haven't you?"

"I thought she'd come back." She was aware of the weakness of her excuse.

His anxiety made him hit out at her. "You've never cared a damn about the child."

"Oh, *Charles*." She was caught off balance by the unfairness of this remark. She said, in a sad, indignant voice, "Am I such a bad mother?" and waited, confidently, for his swift denial.

It did not come. "Sometimes I think you are," he said nastily and replaced the receiver.

Alice could not bear criticism. Now, she took Charles's unkindness more seriously than it had perhaps been intended. She plunged into an abyss of self-hatred and despair. She had neglected Hilary, she was a failure as a mother. Her handsome face took on a downcast, mutinous expression that was remarkably like her daughter's.

To occupy herself, she began to tidy the drawers in the dining-room. She found Aubrey's letter crumpled among the table napkins. Ordinarily, she would not have read it but, at this moment, wallowing as she was in her own vileness, she felt a driving desire to degenerate further. She was a wicked woman, Charles had as good as told her so, why should she stop at reading a private letter?

She read it. The prose was more pretentious than passionate: clearly, it had been written primarily as a literary exercise. But to Alice's distressed mind, the implications seemed clear enough. As she read, she was filled with a painful, rising excitement.

"I worship your mind as dearly as I worship your body. . . . As for Milly, why should my soaring love be confined just because once, long ago, I promised a silly, stupid girl to love and cherish her? There was nothing solemn about that promise, either. It was made in a registry office in a dreary provincial town. Milly wept with her hands folded over her big belly because she was not being sacrificed in a white dress and orange blossom. Her mother wept with shame. There was no gladness, no champagne. Nothing but beer and lamentation. I felt trapped—lonely and afraid in a world I had not made. Can such a sordid ceremony be valid?"

Alice smiled briefly at the absurd, almost legal crispness of the last sentence. Then, crumpling the pages in her hand, her own feelings of guilt were transposed into outraged anger. She had tried so hard to be a mother to this motherless girl and *this* was how she was rewarded. She saw her spasmodic kindness, her good intentions, as a whole-hearted devotion. Throughout lunch, she watched her stepdaughter with smouldering dislike. She could barely wait to confront her with her ingratitude.

Now she repeated, "No *right*? Your father and I are responsible for you. Sometimes responsibility means doing something that may not be in the best of taste."

"It was none of your business." Janet answered her primly. As often happened when she was nervous, her mouth tightened into a mulish sneer. Alice had always found this a peculiarly ugly and unloveable habit: it was associated, for her, with endless scenes of childish temper.

"Do you really think it is none of my business when you behave like a tart?" Seeing the immediate horror in the girl's eyes, her righteous anger mounted. "Is it none of my business when you break up some poor woman's marriage? You think you're clever, don't you, my girl. Hiding behind that girlish innocence. Sweet seventeen! No one would believe it of you, would they? I must say, you took *me* in."

Alice's face was crimson. Her arms made violent, meaningless gestures, strands of hair escaped from their carefully moulded braids.

"I thought butter wouldn't melt in your mouth. To think we trusted you, we thought we'd brought you up to behave decently. Did you never think of the disgrace to *us*. Suppose you had had a baby?"

Distantly, through the mists of excitement that enveloped her, Alice was aware of her own voice shouting in the strident vowels of her childhood and of Janet's wide, stricken eyes. The girl had sunk down on to a hassock and her eyes seemed to grow larger and larger as if they would devour her face.

"You didn't think of that, did you? Or are you still pretending that babies come in the doctor's little black bag?"

Janet went on staring with her huge, dark, stupid eyes. She opened her mouth and no sound came out of it. Finally she murmured, with great effort and in a voice so low that Alice could barely hear it, some form of denial.

Alice tossed her head contemptuously. "Are you trying to tell me that you're still a virgin?"

The brutality of the scene had defeated Janet utterly. The word "virgin" was the final straw: it was a word that had always embarrassed her beyond measure. She covered her face with her hands and wept bitterly. To Alice, her tears seemed an admission of guilt. To some extent, they satisfied and calmed her.

Faintly touched with shame, she **pulled Janet's** hands away from her streaming eyes and offered her a cigarette.

Janet lit it with shaking hand and puffed at it helplessly. They were both silent, weakened with emotion. They avoided each other's eyes.

The front door opened and closed. Auntie had entered the house unnoticed by either of them but now, in the silence they recognised Charles's footsteps. Janet threw her cigarette away and bowed her head. Alice put one hand to her disordered hair.

"Has she come back?"

"No . . ."

Charles looked at his wife and daughter. He said cautiously, scenting trouble, "What's the matter?"

Janet, raising her head, stared at him mutely with suffering eyes. Alice moved towards her with a guilty, protective air.

"It's nothing. A bit of trouble. Nothing important . . ."

She looked, with her hair tumbling round her face and her cheeks glowing with colour, like a great, golden barmaid. Charles was touched, both by her dishevelled appearance and also by her obvious desire to protect Janet.

He said coldly to his daughter. "Really, Janet, I'm ashamed of you. You are thoroughly selfish. We're nearly out of our minds about Hilary and you make a scene. How could you?"

Janet became very pale. Outwardly a dull, insignificant girl, she was inwardly jealous and obscurely passionate. She longed, above all things, to be first with those she loved. When it became apparent that she was not—and she was quick to see a slight—she was given to sudden, ungovernable rages. Quite irrationally, she saw her father's reproof as evidence that she came second to Hilary in his affections. This, curiously, distressed her more than Alice's attack had done.

"What about me?" she cried. "Don't *I* matter? It's

nothing but Hilary, Hilary—I'm sick of the sound of her name. She's a little beast, she stole my letter." Her voice was savage and desolate and childish. "You don't love *me*." She ran from the room. They heard the front door slam.

Alice smiled wanly at her husband. "Oh, dear . . ."

He returned her smile sheepishly and, overcome by a tumult of emotions, she sat down heavily and burst into tears. He went to her and patted her heaving back suspiciously: it was a long time since she had wept in front of him.

"What are we going to do?" she asked, drawing away from his touch, humiliated because he had seen her tears.

He answered her with false cheerfulness. "I've been to the police, they're looking for her. But there's not so much need to worry as we thought. They caught the man this morning. At least she's in no danger from *him*."

The man looked at Hilary and thought: what pretty hair. Bright and shining like the firelight on polished copper.

He could remember far back, farther than most people and his memories were clear. His mind was full of pictures like a photograph album.

He remembered the day when he lay in his crib and stretched out his hands to the copper pan that hung beside the range oven. It was polished and shining with the red-gold flames dancing in the heart of it. He wanted it. He spoke his first, ugly, guttural word.

His grandmother gave him the copper pan to play with. It was cold and cruel to touch. He cried and threw the pan away. His grandmother spoke to him gently, rubbed the pan with her apron and hung it back on its hook where he could look at it.

His grandmother looked after him then: she had long,

white hairs on her chin and her hands were soft and pulpy and crinkled and always damp. She smelt of soap and wet linen. He dozed, in the daytime, to the drip of drying clothes and the squeak of the big, wooden mangle. When his foot hurt, she held it in her hands and rocked him backwards and forwards, crooning to him in the firelight.

One day, his mother was there instead. She opened the door to the rag and bone man and he took away the copper pan with the other shiny kitchen things and the big, brass bedstead where he slept with his grandmother at night when his pain made him lonely or afraid. His mother said: who wants this old rubbish, nothing but work to keep it clean? Feeling her anger, hungry because she had not fed him, he wept sadly, his hands screwed up in front of his eyes. His mother slapped him, saying, stop snivelling, you devil's brat, or I'll give you something to cry for. He was terrified by her red face bending over him. He screamed for his granny in his flat, hideous voice.

His mother put a wet flannel over his face to muffle the noise and to shut out the hateful sight of him. She shook him, her sharp nails digging into his shoulders. Your granny won't come, she said, she's gone away for ever, dead, dead, dead, banging his head against the side of the crib.

Most of his memories were of death, of people dying and leaving him alone. He bent down and touched Hilary's hair. His hands were reverent like the hands of a bishop at a confirmation. He felt love and the longing for love aching in his body like a wound. "Pretty, pretty," he moaned. His hands tightened softly on the little girl's head.

Chapter Five

"It's all right, Auntie," Charles bellowed across the green shaded room. "They've caught the man, the murderer. Sorry if I've disturbed your nap, but I thought you'd like to know."

He had never quite ridden himself of the idea that if only you spoke loudly enough, Auntie would hear. Now, as she bent forward questioningly because she could not clearly see his face, he was irritated at what he suspected, occasionally and unfairly, was an affectation.

He moved closer to her and repeated his message, his lips emphasising the shape of the words.

"All right, all right," she said pettishly. "I'm not blind yet," adding, illogically, "I heard you the first time."

"That's all right, then." He stood upright and mopped his brow. He was tired, the fright had taken it out of him. The pulses throbbed at his temples like angry little hammers.

Auntie was huddled in her chair. He thought he saw her eyelids close. How easily the old fall asleep, he thought, and tip-toed to the door.

Her voice arrested him. She said, indistinctly, "I saw her you know. She must be on her way home."

"Why didn't you say?" he asked, surprised. Alice would be annoyed if she knew. He said, puzzled, "Where did you see her?"

There was a perceptible pause. Then, "She was on the

top of the cliff. I saw her from the beach. She was quite safe. Naturally, I would have gone up after her if it had been necessary." Her voice had a boastful ring and he grinned, hiding his mouth with his hand.

"I bet you would. What were you doing on the beach? Gathering seaweed?"

What a remarkable old creature, he thought indulgently. How many old ladies would scramble along a rough beach at nearly eighty? She must find it dull, after her active life, to be confined to an ageing body. The spirit didn't always grow old at the same pace—hers hadn't, anyway. She was game. She could have shinned up those cliffs if she'd really had to. He was proud of her toughness, her indomitable old age.

He chaffed her good-humouredly. "Come on, tell me what you were doing." He became conscious of a smell of salt and seaweed. There was a garment drying by the fire. "You were paddling," he accused delightedly, "at *your* age!"

She did not respond to his teasing. Her eyes were fixed on him with an unfamiliar look, sly, almost afraid, as if she had something to hide. Her hands fluttered over something in her lap. Curious, he bent forward and saw a toy sailing-boat.

"Surprise for the kids?" he asked.

She thrust the toy behind her back and glared at him. "It's mine," she said. "Mine." He was taken aback by the ferocious intensity in her voice. Poor old girl, he thought, she's going ga-ga.

"Yes," he soothed her. "Of course it is. Did you think I wanted to take it from you?"

"Oh, you fool," she burst out contemptuously. "Just because I'm old, you speak to me as if I were a child—or an animal. You don't know how I feel. You wait till you're old, you'll know what it's like."

94

Concerned, he asked, "What's the matter? Aren't you happy with us? Don't we look after you?"

"Yes, you look after me," she admitted ironically. "You feed me, give me a fire to sit by. But you don't care. When you're young there's an illusion that someone is bound to you, a husband, a lover, a child. . . . It's only when you're old that you can't escape the truth. Then you *know* you're set apart, shut away inside your body and your mind with no one caring how you feel or think. I never knew I was lonely until I grew old."

Her hands trembled together in her lap. For a pitying moment he glimpsed the terror and the sadness that possessed her but he could not understand it. He felt no desire for other people. Loneliness, to him, was freedom. He longed for it like a lover.

"Everyone is alone. You don't have to be old to know that. There's no comfort in other people," he said wearily, feeling suddenly worn out, finished. His body was a life sentence, it gave him claustrophobia.

"The Church," he said with difficulty. "Faith might help. . . ."

"I don't believe in God," she said. "A fairy story for weaklings."

For a moment, her eyes brightened, she sat more stiffly in her chair. But it was only a temporary recovery: almost immediately she slumped back into a hunched, defeated position. When Charles spoke to her, she made no response and fell, quite suddenly asleep, whimpering a little, a stream of pale dribble running unheeded from the corner of her mouth. With surprise he saw, for the first time clearly, that she was really very old. In the last few years she must have declined without his noticing it. Up to this moment he had, he realised, thought of her not as she was but as he had, as a young man, known her. Then, when her

95

deafness was only partial, she had flourished a hearing-aid like a decoration and been an asset to any dinner party. She had been Charles's fascinating aunt, the wit, the monumental old character. At nearly sixty she had tramped Europe, an intrepid water-colourist, with one hundred pounds and a hot-water bottle in her ruck-sack.

Now he looked at the ruin and thought, without much pity: poor old girl, but I suppose we all come to it in the end. An indignity, perhaps, but is there any use in whining? Some people were luckier, though—for himself, he prayed passionately for a quick death, no dragging years of use-lessness.

As he left the house to look for Hilary it began to rain, big, pattering drops like a summer storm.

Hilary shook her head violently and, dropping his hands to his sides, the man stepped backwards.

"You should be more careful," he said. "I knew a little girl got stuck in one of those pipes. She was playing a game and she got stuck inside."

She looked up at him, her hands gripping the edge of the pipe. "What happened to her?" she asked curiously.

"I don't know. Her friends ran away and left her. They didn't tell anyone. They were afraid that if they did, they'd get into trouble. So they left her and pretended that they'd been somewhere else all afternoon."

Hilary nodded. She was not surprised at what seemed to her entirely natural behaviour. Her legs felt cramped inside the pipe. "I feel stuck," she said, horrified. The man smiled kindly and bending, hauled her out. Her dress was crumpled and covered with red dust. He brushed her down with his hands, muttering softly to himself. Then he spat on a corner of his dirty handkerchief and wiped the rust from her hands and face. When he had finished, he looked at her critically and smiled.

Then he sat down with his back against the sun-warmed pipe and took out a hunk of bread and cheese. He hacked at it with a penknife, singing a tune under his breath. He ignored Hilary completely.

She stood and watched him, shifting from one foot to the other. She sighed deeply. Nothing interesting was going to happen after all. It was a dull and pedestrian climax to the excitement that had seized her inside the pipe. She sidled up to the man and stood beside him, breathing heavily.

He said, without looking up, "Do you want something to eat, girlie?"

"Yes, please." She sat beside him and watched his thin fingers tear the bread into two. He gave her half the bread and a piece of dry, cheese rind. She ate it quickly, stuffing it into her mouth and swallowing it in lumps. His eyes flickered briefly over her face before he went back to the business of his own meal. He ate daintily, rolling the soft bread into grey, smooth pellets and pecking at them like a bird. As he swallowed, his long hair fell forward, curving across his face with a smooth, glossy motion like a bird's wings folding.

Hilary watched him with fear that felt like ecstasy. She sat quite still so as not to disturb him, her knees drawn up to her chin. When he was done, he brushed the crumbs from his coat and turned his head. He stared at Hilary with dark, mournful, unblinking eyes until she felt as if she were drowning in them. She could not look away.

He smiled, a gentle, loving smile. "You're a funny little girl, aren't you?"

"Why?" she asked expectantly. Delicious shivers ran through her body.

97

"A pretty little girl," he continued without answering her, "but are you a sensible little girl, I wonder?" He cocked his head on one side and regarded her inquiringly. "I think you are," he said. "I think so, yes, yes, yes." He bobbed his head jerkily like a Jack-in-the-box and Hilary felt the laughter forcing itself up inside her. She clapped her hands over her mouth.

He leaned back comfortably against the pipe and laid his hand on her knee. Dreamily, his eyes half-closed, he went on, "I like little girls, but not when they run away or scream. I can't bear it when they cry. You wouldn't run away or scream, would you?"

His eyes sought hers and she shook her head dumbly. She was afraid when he put his face close to hers and she said, to divert his attention. "Where do you live?" It was the first thing that came into her head.

"Over there." He waved his hand in the direction of the caravans, a field away. Beyond them, on the coastal road, Hilary could see the roofs of the cars winking in the sun.

"Wally lives there, too," she said. "He promised to show me his caravan one day."

"Do you want to come and see where I live?" He made the offer casually but as soon as he had spoken the idea seemed to catch his fancy and he went on in an urgent, coaxing voice, "I've got a bird. A soft, little, yellow bird. You can feed it if you like. It feeds out of my hand. It won't be frightened of you if you're nice and quiet."

He stood up and lifted her to her feet. His hands were hard and trembled against her body. She wanted to go with him and yet she was afraid to go. She shrank from him and, at the same time, longed for him to enfold her with his love. Irresolute, she put her finger in her mouth and stared at him.

"Come now," he said, and took her hand.

"*No.*"

The wind blew in her face, the sky grew dark. She remembered Poppet, walking along the front under the perilous, cold sky; Peregrine; the Devil's cloven hoof. Fear beat like wings in her throat and burst from her mouth in a single shouted word.

His voice was thin. "You're afraid."

Somehow, she knew that was the danger point. She forced herself to stay still, to look up at him. "I'm not," she said. "Only just now, I have to go. I'll come another time, if I may, but not to-day. It's very important," she went on, extemporising wildly, "you see my grandfather is coming to tea this afternoon. He's very rich and he loves me a lot, much, much more than Peregrine although he's much nicer than I am really. *You* know Peregrine, don't you? You saw him the other day, at Uncle Jack's. My grandfather is going to leave all his money to me when he dies and not to Peregrine, so I must be there when he comes, mustn't I? But I'll come to-morrow, I promise. I'd like to see your bird. Good-bye."

She held out her hand. He did not take it. He did not move. He watched her with a surprised look on his thin face. Then his eyes narrowed. "I remember *you*," he said and took an undecided step towards her.

Slow drops of rain began to fall: one splashed on the top of her head and trickled through her hair on to her scalp, like syrup. Very slowly, she began to walk backwards, watching him. He made no move towards her. When she was a few yards away from him, she turned and walked towards the cliff. She wanted to run, her spirit raced ahead of her on desperate feet. He had said: I don't like little girls who run away or scream. She must walk slowly so he would think she was not afraid. Her

99

tongue felt thick and swollen and filled her mouth: if she tried to scream, no sound would come out of it. Dear God and Jesus, if You let me get home or, if that's too difficult for You, if You let me get to the Downs, I'll be good always, I'll do what I'm told, I'll do my homework, I promise, for Thine is the Kingdom, the Power and the Glory, for ever and ever, Amen.

No prayer goes unanswered if you pray with your heart, Nanny had said. She put all her strength into her prayer, seeing God like Father Christmas, robed in red, sitting on a cloud.

She reached the edge of the field and came out on to the cliff top by the shelter. Then she turned, slowly and deliberately, and saw him looking after her. It was raining hard, now, but he stood quite still. He looked sad and lonely, she thought, and she was suddenly ashamed because she had run away from him. He was unhappy because she had left him, she knew. The thought made her feel pleased and important. She waved her hand to him kindly and after a moment he raised his arm in reply, holding it stiffly in the air like a benediction.

"I'll come to-morrow," she called and the wind blew suffocatingly into her open mouth. She looked along the cliff top towards home and saw her father walking towards her. He walked with long strides, his big body top-heavy on his thin, old man's legs, his coat collar turned up round his neck. He was too far away for her to see his face.

At the sight of him, her legs felt weak and her eyes misted over. Darting into the shelter, she knelt on the slatted seat and gazed through the glass at the swelling sea. The rain was making black, pitted holes in the water. She began to sing, "There is a green hill far away," in a high, tuneless voice. The hymn answered her emotional need and, as she reached the lines, "There was no other good enough, to pay the price of sin," her voice quivered and failed. A gush of warm tears overflowed her eyes and she felt cleansed and purified. When her father came into the shelter, she looked up at him and said, in an indifferent voice, "Oh, it's you."

"My little girl," he said in a hoarse voice. Lifting her bodily from the seat, he buried his face roughly in her neck. She wriggled and he set her down, holding tightly on to her hand.

"Never do this again, never, never," he said. His nails dug into her wrist. His strange, hot face, the pale tears in his eyes, embarrassed her beyond bearing. She pulled away from his hand and when he would not let her go, bent her head and bit his wrist. She heard his cry of pain and saw his face like a great, red sun swimming towards her. With an inarticulate wail, she ran towards the cliff edge. When she came to the drop, she turned and put her hands before her eyes, hiding from his anger and the enormous wickedness of her deed.

She looked as if she were cringing from an expected blow and Charles, who had never struck his children, was deeply moved.

"My poor little love," he murmured, "my poor baby."

Alice had recently been reading a book on child psychology. She had carefully rehearsed her scene with Hilary beforehand.

"Now dear. I think we must have a little talk, don't you?"

Hilary, bathed and fed, shuffled in her chair before the nursery fire. Her eyes were bent sullenly on the floor. Alice felt that the little talk would be better staged if she had the child on her lap and, sitting on a low stool, tried to draw

Hilary towards her. Hilary pulled away, pursing her lips and shaking her head. Annoyed, Alice clasped her hands round her knees and addressed her with less sweetness than she had intended.

"You're quite old enough to be talked to like a sensible person. It was naughty of you to run away, but that isn't the important thing. What is important, is why you did it. Do you know why?"

Hilary stared at her blankly.

"I'm going to tell you why. And you must listen carefully because if you understand *why* you ran away, then you won't want to do anything like it ever again. Now—sometimes you are a rather silly little girl. You think Mummy doesn't love you. It isn't true, of course, but all the same you sometimes want to punish Mummy for not loving you. You thought, to-day, that if you ran away she would be frightened and unhappy and it would pay her out. That was why you ran away, wasn't it?"

Alice was pleased with her explanation. She felt it showed a thorough understanding of the child mind. When Hilary did not immediately respond, she wondered whether the use of the third person had bewildered her. She leaned forward and spoke more directly. "You ran away to frighten me, didn't you?"

Hilary shook her head and said in a bored voice, "No. I didn't."

Vexed at what seemed deliberate obtuseness, Alice insisted. "It would be better if you told me the truth. Let's try again. You ran away to make me unhappy, didn't you?"

Hilary's eyes sought hers with a faint, imploring look. For a moment, Alice had her doubts and then, when the child answered, "I don't know. Perhaps," they were easily dispelled. It was not a complete admission but it was good enough: it laid the foundation for the rest of her argument.

"That's better, dear. Now, listen to me. We all love you so there is not the smallest reason to be afraid of *that*. I love both my children. You and Peregrine. Sometimes you are a little jealous of Peregrine. Do you know what that means?"

Hilary breathed heavily through her nostrils. Alice knelt on the floor beside her. She was curiously excited. She wanted to caress the child but desisted.

She said carefully, "Well, dear, it means that sometimes you wish you were a boy. Because you think I love Peregrine best. Sometimes you even wish he wasn't there at all so that you could have Mummy all to yourself. Isn't that true?"

Hilary's brow cleared. She even gently smiled as if this were a simple and perfectly impersonal question like three-times-eight or who burned the cakes? She said helpfully, "Sometimes I wish he would die."

Recoiling, Alice searched her face for some signs of sly, intentional cleverness. Seeing the unpretending truth, she cried loudly, "Hilary, don't you love your little brother?"

Hilary was aware that she had disappointed her mother. "I suppose so," she answered, her doubtful eyes watching Alice's face. Then, with a pleading smile, she thrust out her arm so that the pink flannel fell away and pointed to a red mark on her baby flesh. "Look," she said with a faint, placating whine, "I burned myself, too. We were only playing a game."

"Nonsense," said Alice strongly, "Do you expect me to believe that?" Her head was throbbing. How bad a mother had she been for her children to hate one another? She longed to hurt this stupid, passionless child who had exposed her failure so plainly. "It is very wicked of you to talk like that," she said in a low, spiteful voice. "It was very wicked of you to hurt Peregrine. Mummy only had Peregrine so that you wouldn't be a lonely little girl without any brothers or sisters. Mummy suffered terribly when he was born and all her pain was for you." Her eyes filled with tears. "Your little brother is a holy trust," she whispered.

Hilary burst into loud, raucous weeping. When soft, loving arms were folded round her, she did not resist, but clung tightly to her tormentor. Rocking her gently, murmuring soothing words, Alice felt satisfied and calm. She had achieved her object, not the direct pleasure of causing pain, but the resulting fulfilment of her urgent maternal need—a positive response from her unresponsive child. She knew she had been cruel and, later, this would disgust and shame her, but now, in her assured position of comforter, she was rich and secured against the world. Drawing the child deeper into her embrace, she said softly, "It's all right, darling. Mummy loves you. Do you love Mummy?"

"Yes, yes," Hilary moaned, her hot face buried in the scented breasts.

Such an emotional exchange was unusual between mother and daughter for both were deeply shy: Hilary's admission aroused in Alice a storm of proud, possessive love. "My own darling," she murmured, and with a consciously tender gesture kissed the defeated brow.

Hilary woke in fear. She crawled up from sleep through a dark tunnel and, waking to the light, was unable to remember what had frightened her.

The storm had blown itself out and a pale sun filled the room. Through the open window, she heard the late holidaymakers on the Downs, their voices ugly and unfamiliar with lazy, suburban vowels. Come here now, this minute, or I'll give you what-for. In the high, blue sky, she watched a sea-gull floating, turning in the sun. Idly, she floated with it, for a moment she felt the warm wind on her own breast. She thought, who am I? Wonderingly, she touched the cool flesh of her arm.

She remembered the man, a terror, haunting her dreams, and turned over on to her face.

A little later the curtains were closed and the room was dim. Peregrine, in his night clothes, was standing by her bed. As she opened her eyes, she surprised a secret expression on his face as if he had been watching her for a long time. She hated the thought that he had seen her asleep and sat upright, saying, "I wasn't really asleep, you know. Just thinking."

He took her lie without a flicker of disbelief. "Daddy and I brought you a present," he recited hoarsely and fumbled beneath his pyjama jacket.

The tabby kitten danced, stiff-legged, across the counterpane and stalked Hilary's delighted hand among the bed-clothes. Half-away, looking into the sea-green eyes, Hilary thought, who am I? A cat, a wild cat, a tiger in the undergrowth. She touched it. Its fur was so soft that it was like nothing else in the world. It fled joyously to the end of the bed and crouched flat-bellied with twitching tail.

"Is it really mine? Then I'll call it Hilary."

He frowned. "You can't. It's a girls name."

"Why not? All right, then, it isn't mine. You said it was a present."

"It is," he pleaded. "It's yours, really. I bought it with my own shilling. You can call it what you like. Only it can't stay here now. Daddy said it must live in the kitchen because it might do things under the bed."

She might have known there would be a catch in it. Nothing was ever freely given. There was a rotten core to all delight.

"Take it away, then," she said stonily.

He stammered, "I h-have to. It's not m-my fault. I wasn't supposed to show you now at all. Mummy said wait till the morning. She said you were asleep." His voice became confident and injured.

She relented. "All right. You'd better take it. We'll fetch it in the morning when we wake up."

He departed, the kitten bouncing on his shoulder, the cord of his dressing-gown trailing on the floor. When he returned, he advanced boldly to the end of her bed and asked, "Did you like my present? You didn't say thank you."

"Why do you always have to be *thanked*?" she asked irritably.

He answered stubbornly. "You should always say thank you when someone gives you a present. It isn't polite not to."

She said, in a mocking voice, "Thank you, dear Peregrine."

His lips shook. "Not like that," he protested with dignity.

He stood beside her, a thin little boy in a handed-down dressing-gown that was too small, even for him. Wrists like matches stuck out of frayed sleeves, there was a sore, swollen patch on his lip. Suddenly remorseful, she knelt and beat her head solemnly on the counterpane, intoning, "Thank you, O Great One, O Bringer of Rich Gifts."

His giggles became uncontrollable. He stuffed his sleeve in his mouth. "I said you were asleep," he said. "I promised not to wake you up."

She slid under the bedclothes and lay still, ankles crossed, hands folded on her breast. Seeing the delight on his face, her heart flowed over with kindness. "You can come into my bed if you like."

He took off his dressing-gown and hung it neatly over the iron rail at the head of his own bed. Then he climbed into the warm place she had made for him.

Fixing her eyes on the ceiling, she said casually, "Does your mouth hurt?"

He felt it tenderly. "Only if I touch it."

She said awkwardly, "I didn't mean to hurt you.·'

"I expect I deserved it," he said humbly. Their hands met and stickily clasped.

He said fearfully, "Where did you go?"

Her heart leapt. "I saw *Him* again," she confided rapidly. "I climbed the cliff and played on the pipes. Then he gave me some bread. He lives in a caravan. He wanted me to go home with him and see his bird."

"Did you?" he asked, impressed.

"No."

He continued eagerly, "I wish I'd been there. Would he have taken me too?"

She considered this and smiled triumphantly. "I don't expect so, not for a minute. He only likes little girls. He told me so."

"But you could have *asked* him to take me. I expect he would if you'd asked him. I've never seen inside a caravan. It's not fair, you get all the fun."

Had it been fun? She said spitefully, "You'd have been afraid to go. You're always afraid of things."

He said meekly, "I'd have tried not to be. Did you see his horns?"

"No. He didn't have any. I don't believe he *is* the Devil." Her voice rose. She felt an upsurge of wild relief as if, by her loud denial, she could strip him of his vile importance, reduce him to no more than an old man, mumbling his bread in a field. That was all he was, really, someone to be whispered about, the stranger you were not supposed to talk to.

By his next words he killed her faint hope forever. "Perhaps he only didn't want *you* to see. Of course, he can make himself into any shape he likes . . ."

"Then if it's true, if he really *is* . . ." She could not bring herself to finish the sentence. Instead, she concluded, "You didn't tell Janet. Or Mummy, or anyone . . ."

"Oh no," he said gravely. "I didn't tell *them*. It wouldn't have been any use."

He was so calm about it, so free from the kind of awed excitement that would have hinted at deliberate tale-telling, that Hilary was convinced. He had tossed his belief at her quite casually, so sure himself of its rightness that it was impossible to question it.

Shivering, Hilary pressed herself against the warm angles of his body. She felt herself to be poised above a dark and terrible abyss.

She said, "I don't suppose I shall see him again, do you? But anyway, I won't go anywhere without you, ever again." She ended, fearfully, "And you mustn't go anywhere without *me*."

He moved restlessly beneath her clutching hands. "You're hurting me," he complained. "I want to go back to my own bed."

She knew he meant it, he liked his comfort. And she could not bear to be left alone. "Don't go." She searched for a bribe. "If you stay in my bed, you can choose the name for the kitten. So in a way it'll be your kitten as well as mine."

She half-regretted the offer as soon as it was made: he would have been contented, she knew, with a far less magnificent gesture.

As she had feared, he clinched the bargain immediately. His nature, though nobler than hers, was also more forthright: he had a clear eye for his own advantage.

"I shall call her Moppet," he said firmly, "and if I stay you mustn't poke me."

"I won't," she agreed meekly. She lay carefully still until he was asleep beside her, holding her body rigidly apart from his. When his breathing grew heavier, she moved cautiously closer to him, drawing his sleeping arm across her chest. Locked against his familiar body, she knew comfort and safety. He was with her, he shared her loneliness. While they were together, she need not be afraid.

When she ran from the house, leaving it, she assured herself passionately, for ever, Janet had forgotten both her coat and her handbag so that when she reached the town she was not only wet but almost, though not quite, moneyless. The pocket of her dress revealed a sixpence, a threepenny bit and a halfpenny, presumably the change from a 'bus ride. This discovery plunged her into the deepest gloom and self-recrimination: what an inefficient fool she was, how did she imagine she could make a gesture of defiance on ninepence halfpenny?

She sat in a shelter on the front, alone except for a pair of shop girls in plastic mackintoshes giggling in a corner, and stared at the sea. Her wet dress clung coldly to her body but she was in the elevated state occasionally produced by violent agitation and unaware of physical discomfort.

She began to examine her relationship with Aubrey in the light of the interpretation Alice had placed on it. At first, Alice's belief that she and Aubrey were lovers had seemed the quite unwarranted assumption of an evil-

minded woman. Janet had felt indignation, shame, and
above all, surprise. Now, her innocence gone for ever, she
saw that her stepmother's conclusion had been entirely
reasonable. She thought, not being of a sufficiently self-
deceptive nature to persuade herself that *her* case was
different: presumably it is more likely, if people love, that
they are lovers.

Having admitted this point, she began to feel young and
unsophisticated. Her sins had been so childish. She hated
Aubrey for having put her in a false position. She hated
Alice for making her look a fool. More than anything else
she hated Hilary. Angry tears stung her eyelids.

The sun came out. Rainbows of oil shimmered in the
puddles on the promenade, the gilded dome of the pier
pavilion reflected the bright rays with tawdry splendour.
Frail as an echo, the synthetic music of the Fun Fair came
to her on the wind.

The front became crowded. In the dying afternoon,
children, released from the boredom of boarding house, and
ice-cream parlour, clattered their pails on the beach. People
were coming out of the cinema. Arm in arm, they strolled
in pairs, their faces shining in the damp, clean air. She
thought: everyone is happier than I am, and walked, self-
consciously alone, on to the pier.

Along the length of the pier, the fishermen leaned on the
rails, the deck beside them littered with canvas bags and jars
of squirming bait. In the centre of an interested circle of
spectators, a conger eel wriggled and snapped, its red mouth
open. Grinning, a man bent forward and hacked at the back
of its head with a clumsy knife.

Averting her eyes, she leaned over the rail and looked
at the green water sucking at the barnacled supports of
the pier. A voice called her and she turned to see one of
her school friends, a girl she had not seen since their last

term. Wearing an embroidered peasant blouse, her hair knotted in a pony tail she had been walking with her boy friend who now waited a few yards away, affecting indifference to this encounter. Both girls were embarrassed by his presence and as they talked, they darted shy glances at his profile. They talked about the girls they had both known: what had happened to Bernice, to Ann, to the Italian girl who had been going to take a course at R.A.D.A.? The brief spurt of interest they had both felt on first seeing each other flickered and died like a candle flame in a gust of wind.

Sheila said, "Well, I must be going now. . . . It's too absurd, really, that you should *still* be here. London's such fun, you've no idea, dances and parties. . . ." Her eyes shone like glass beads in the sun.

"We must see each other," Janet ventured, feeling dowdy.

"That would be *marvellous*. If you come to Town, just give me a ring. Cheery-bye for now."

With the same enthusiasm with which she had first greeted Janet, Sheila left her. She thrust her hand through her boy's crooked arm. Brightly, she smiled. The boy gave a shy grin. He was very young, not yet twenty and his navy blazer with pink piping was too small for him.

They walked towards the shore. Sheila's high heels clicked on the uneven boards. The boy walked jerkily, trying to match his steps to hers.

Janet shivered and looked at her watch. It was after six. She walked slowly, anxious not to catch up with Sheila and her boy who were strolling with their arms round each other's waists. Unfortunately, they stopped at a seat and she was forced to pass them. As she did so, she quickened her steps and pretended an intense interest in the view from the opposite side of the pier. She knew this would not deceive them: Sheila, enlarging on the incident to her friends, would say that Janet Bray had deliberately followed them.

This encounter increased her sense of isolation. She was a natural outcast, a butt. She had no friends, her family did not understand her. She saw herself growing old, unmarried at thirty, her life wasting. Shrouded in a delicious melancholy, she walked home. She had nowhere else to go.

Creeping up the stairs, she met Alice on the landing. She had just closed the door of Auntie's room and her expression was forbidding.

"Oh, it's you, is it." She was as disconcerted as Janet. Their eyes met guiltily.

"Is she back?" asked Janet in an exhausted voice. She leaned heavily on the banisters, anxious to appear worn out and pitiable.

Alice nodded. "Asleep. She knows about the murder."

"*I* didn't tell her."

"I didn't say you did. It's *her* fault." Frowning, Alice jerked her head at Auntie's door. "That awful old woman."

"She'll upset Peregrine," said Janet, anxious to put Hilary in the worst light possible. "She's bound to tell him. She enjoys frightening him." She went on hastily to avoid discussing the matter. "I must change my dress."

"You're wet," said Alice in a surprised but uninterested tone.

"Soaked." Janet elaborated with childish pathos. "Soaked right through to my skin."

"Of course—you were looking for Hilary," said Alice in a softer tone.

Janet did not disabuse her. She went into her room.

Alice hesitated for a moment and then followed her. She closed the door.

"Janet . . ."

"Yes?"

There was a certain respect in Alice's face and manner. Her voice was hushed and conspiratorial. "I was unkind, earlier. I'm sorry. If . . . if you should find yourself in trouble, you would tell me, wouldn't you?"

Janet did not immediately understand her. When she did, she was too ashamed of her own innocence to tell the truth. She looked at the floor with a guilty expression and said, "Yes, yes of course I would tell you."

Alice, looking for the morning newspaper, had discovered it in Auntie's room. Since the afternoon, Auntie had progressed through despair to indifference. She no longer cared what became of her and despised herself for having, in her weakness, been afraid of Alice. Who was she, anyway? A presumptuous, working-class chit who had bettered herself by marriage.

This state of mind led her, inevitably, into imprudence. When she confessed to Alice that Hilary had found the newspaper where she had carelessly left it, she did so with a haughty lack of apology that breathed a fine, social arrogance.

Alice behaved rather better. She said it was unfortunate but could not be helped. It would not do to be too angry with Auntie: she might leave her money elsewhere.

After dinner, when Janet had gone to bed, she spent her anger on Charles. "She's an irresponsible old woman. Fancy allowing Hilary to see the newspaper! God knows what she made of it."

"She'll forget." Charles, putting aside the newspaper, looked up reluctantly.

"Not *this*. She'll make the most of it. She's got a ghoulish mind. In a few days she'll persuade herself that she saw the whole thing at least. You know what she is!"

Charles sighed. "Don't make too much of it, dear." He saw that she was working herself into a nervous state and said soothingly, "I agree it's a pity."

Alice continued dramatically, "It's more than a pity. She won't keep it to herself. Janet says she's bound to tell Peregrine. And he's such a sensitive little chap. Heaven knows what horrors she'll tell him. She'll frighten him out of his wits. He must be sent away. . . ."

"My dear girl, are you out of your mind?" He saw, by her angry reddening, that this was quite the wrong line to pursue. He ended, awkwardly, "Where to, anyway? After all, school starts next week."

"He could go to your brother. He likes the farm. And it would do him more harm to hear about this dreadful business than to miss a few days school. He'll listen to anything Hilary tells him. He must be got out of it."

Her face lit with crusading fervour. If Charles refused to see the danger, then it was up to her to act, to save Peregrine from contamination. "He must go to-morrow." She added, in a significant voice, "Janet can take him. I'd like her to leave Henstable too, for a while. There are reasons. . . ." She had no intention of telling Charles what those reasons were, but she could not resist making a mystery out of it.

Charles shrugged his shoulders. He was tired: he had no inclination for decision and practicalities. Indeed, he could not bring himself to think the matter of any importance: it seemed as if a veil had been drawn between him and the world.

Alice said indignantly, "Charles, you aren't listening . . ."

"I'm sorry," he said. "I'm not feeling too well. I'll

DEVIL BY THE SEA

telephone Edward this evening. Of course, you're perfectly right."

"You really think so?" Alice was surprised at his easy acquiescence and a little sorry that she had been so insistent. She became aware that she did not really think it necessary for Peregrine to go and that she had relied on Charles's making light of the matter. She said, abashed, "They need only go for a week."

Standing, she adjusted her hair in the looking-glass above the mantelpiece. She was flushed and looked very attractive and alive; emotion became her. Glancing at Charles, she thought: how different we are. There are not so many years between us and yet he looks quite old and finished, a dry stick. She wondered, with fear: can he be really ill?

He was looking into the fire. He said, "Alice, do you ever feel cut off? From other people, I mean." He frowned into the flames, trying to find the right words to reach her. It seemed suddenly tremendously important that she should understand him. "It's as if we were each enclosed in a bubble. When I had pneumonia that time, it was like that. You know the other people are there, you can see them, talk to them, but that's all there ever is. So much goes on that you can never understand and the awful thing, the really terrible thing, is that you don't *want* to understand, you don't care." He regarded her earnestly with shy, soft eyes. Seeing the frozen look on her face, his hope died.

"I really don't know what you're talking about," she said, bridling. "I'm sure *I* care about other people. And understand them, too. It only needs a little imagination."

"But aren't you ever lonely?" he cried. He hesitated on the verge of telling her about his immediate worry; his treacherous heart.

115

Then she gave a high, indignant laugh. "Really, Charles, you *are* morbid. You're tired, that's the matter with you. You think too much about yourself, worrying over your health like a stupid old woman." She went on in a forced, motherly tone, proud of her ability to manage him when he was in a silly mood, "Pull yourself together and be sensible, now. I'll make you a nice, hot drink."

Chapter Six

It was announced at breakfast that Hilary was to spend the morning with her father. The barely concealed anxiety with which her reaction was awaited, coupled with the air of mystery and bustle that had pervaded the house since the early morning, might have caused a more perceptive child to wonder at this sudden "treat". However, Hilary, who appeared to be in a dulled and downcast mood—not, Charles thought, simply sulky but rather *absent* as if she were inwardly and completely occupied with some problem of her own—merely expressed her satisfaction at Peregrine's exclusion from the expedition and went upstairs, as she was told, to put on a clean frock.

Charles said, "Is there anything wrong with her?" He spoke in an undertone because Peregrine, who was a slow eater, was still buttering his first slice of toast.

"With Hilary?" Alice stirred an extra spoonful of sugar into her coffee. She had a very sweet tooth. "Why? Was she behaving oddly?"

"No. I just thought she looked . . ." The words faded in the moted sunlight falling on the breakfast table. He stared at the brown, smiling sides of the earthenware coffee jug, wondering exactly how she had looked, what it had been that made him uneasy about her. "A little tired, perhaps," he finished, relaxing and rolling his napkin into his ring.

"It's just one of her moods. She's a bad-tempered little

pig." Janet was in a mood herself. Her expression was dark and lowering. She did not want to be Peregrine's nursemaid for a week. She had expected Alice's kindness of the night before to open the gates to a new and happier era: she resented being sent away like a naughty child.

Alice ignored her remark. "I expect she's just tired," she said to her husband, adding in a meaningful tone, "after yesterday."

"Early to bed, to-night." Charles stood, smiling at his wife. He kissed her tidily on the side of her unpainted, morning mouth.

"Come along, Daddy," cried Hilary from the door. "We don't want to be late, do we?"

She wore her best dress of yellow muslin, seed pearls, patent leather shoes.

"Really, Hilary, what a get-up." Alice clashed her cup in the saucer. "You're not going to a party."

Hilary glared. "It doesn't matter." She twirled round in the doorway.

Relieved, Charles saw that her trouble, whatever it was, had vanished. She had shed her small burden with her grubby frock and now appeared simply and childishly excited at the prospect of an outing. She grinned at her father and thrust her hand into his.

"Good-bye," they cried. The front door slammed. Draped in his damask napkin, Peregrine waved mournfully from the dining-room window. The day was bright and glittering, the hard, salty wind blew in their faces. On the Downs, the coloured kites tore into the sky.

"Look," Hilary shouted. "The kites . . ." She seized a whippy stick from the hedge and leaned on it, walking with an exaggerated limp. "Old didee, old didee," she chanted in an exhilarated voice, "old didee."

"What's that, what's that?" Charles caught up with her

and bent his head. She looked up, ashamed. "Just a game." She flung the stick into the gutter. "A baby's game. I only play it because Peregrine likes it." She strutted importantly beside him. "Daddy, what are we going to do to-day?"

Her plain, freckled face was illuminated. Charles pitied her precarious happiness. The morning was bound to end for her in shame and disappointment. She would find out soon enough that the present arrangement had not been made for her pleasure but merely to get her out of the way. She had not been told of Peregrine's departure because she would make a scene—and a scene had to be avoided at all costs because Peregrine must be kept calm. He was inclined to be train sick.

"We're going to the shop," he said carefully. "And then perhaps we'll get a taxi and go to an auction."

"That's not much of a treat," she said flatly. "Can we go the Dairymaid and have an ice cream?"

"We'll see. If you're good." Then, because she was an ugly little girl and because he guessed that life had not been and never would be as easy for her as it was for her brother, he said, "I expect it can be managed."

Cooper's taxi was bouncy and old. The seats were blown up with air and billowed round them like feather pillows. Hilary sang to herself, ate the liquorice allsorts that Miss Hubback had given her and watched the back of Mr. Cooper's neck. It was as red as a boiled crab and bristled with sharp black hairs.

They drove back from the auction, along the coastal road. As they approached Grey's Field, Hilary stood up and shouted, "Oh, stop, do stop, Mr. Cooper. The gipsies, look."

There was no alternative. The first caravan was half-way

across the road, blocking their passage. Cooper bumped off the road and halted on dusty grass.

Charles said impatiently, "What's all this?"

Hilary turned a glowing face towards him. "They're leaving. They've got to. They're being sent away. Wally told me. The man the field belongs to doesn't want them any more."

"Nasty, dirty, thieving lot," said Cooper.

"Poor gipsies," said Hilary in a sentimental tone.

"I don't suppose they mind, really," Charles comforted her. "Gipsies are used to wandering all over the place."

She wriggled her body inside her dress. "Wally says, if they don't go, they'll drive them away with sticks and guns. Bang, shee-ow." Hilary stretched out her arms and screamed like a dive bomber.

"Bloodthirsty, aren't you?" said Cooper.

Charles was slightly revolted by this sudden change in her attitude. "Go and watch them if you like," he conceded in a cold voice.

She left the car and ran, yellow skirt flying, through a gap in the hedge and into the field. The coarse grass streamed like water before the wind, and high above her head the long line of poplars turned their leaves, like silver-bellied fish, to the sun.

There were about ten caravans in all. Men shouted at straining horses. Harness creaked and jangled, dogs, running belly to earth beneath the wheels, yelped hysterically. The gipsies were drably dressed and dirty but their caravans were romantic and magical. Gilded and painted, embossed with swags of golden grapes, they scraped their marvellous sides on the gate posts. Through the open doors at the back, Hilary saw swinging crockery, painted panels, dark women.

Before such splendour, her heart rejoiced and sang. Here

was beauty, strange and wild. She longed to be going with them, over the hills and far away.

"What are you doing here?" said Wally, behind her. "You'll catch it."

"Does your mother know you're out?" said one of his friends and gave a high, crowing laugh.

"My Daddy does. He's waiting for me in the car."

The four boys gathered round Hilary suspiciously like strange dogs. They wore jeans, check woollen shirts and furry Davy Crockett hats. They carried sticks. One of them, the jester, swiped at Wally's leg.

"Here, cut it out, will you?" said Wally fiercely.

Hilary stood close to Wally and gazed at him admiringly. Her day was crowned. He was her star, her love.

"Wouldn't you like to be a gipsy, Wally?" she breathed.

Wally hesitated. He shared Hilary's romantic feelings about the gipsies. He had a tender, poetic soul but would have died rather than let it be known.

"*Wouldn't you like to be a gipsy, Wally dear?*" mimicked the biggest boy.

Wally frowned terribly. "Me? Jesus Christ!" He poked Hilary in the ribs and roared with laughter. "Fatty," he said.

At the end of the procession of caravans came an open cart loaded with sacks and pulled by a piebald pony, a prancing dandy in scarlet blinkers. On the top of the sack sat two men and a gipsy child. Her hair was long and ringleted, her eyes like black prunes. She was waving frantically at someone they could not see, a handkerchief held in her small, brown hand. The cart lurched in the ruts and she fell forward on her knees. Neither of the men made any move to help her and she rolled over the tail of the cart and sprawled on the ground. There was a shout of laughter, the cart rumbled on.

The boys giggled. The little girl scrambled to her feet, spat out a dreadful word and ran after the cart. She caught at the end of it, tripped, was dragged along on her knees. She screamed thinly.

"Jesus Christ! Cut it out," shouted Wally.

The gipsy's casual laughter floated back on the wind. One of the men, a scarf knotted on his bare chest, leaned forward lazily and hauled her to safety. She regained her seat, weeping, and immediately continued her desperate waving. Her little hand fluttered poignantly like a trapped bird. The cart moved on, into the road, vanished from sight.

The children were violently excited by this episode. One of the boys stood on his head and went red in the face.

"Did you hear what she *said*?" cried Hilary. "Wasn't it rude? She said . . ."

"Shut up," said Wally virtuously. "She don't know no better. There won't half be a row if your Mum hears you say that."

"I say worse things than that sometimes," said Hilary proudly.

"She was saying good-bye to *him*," said the boy who had stood on his head. He waved his stick. The man was standing on the other side of the gate, hidden from their sight until now by the gipsy cavalcade. He stood very still, looking through the gateway after the gipsy child, shrunken inside his enormous coat.

Hilary saw him with excited dread. She clutched at Wally's arm. "I told you I'd seen the Devil, didn't I?" She gave a wild, choked laugh and, flinging out her free arm, pointed to the man. "There he is, that's him," she screamed.

The jester laughed his high, crowning laugh. "Old devil, old devil," he chanted.

The man looked in their direction. His face was thin and white. He did not move.

"That's only Dotty Jim," said Wally, scowling. He glanced uneasily at Hilary. "He's mad. Sometimes, when the moon's full, he barks like a dog. I've heard him." He pushed her away roughly. "Don't maul me about," he said.

"Old devil," shouted the biggest boy. "See him run." He picked up a smooth, white stone and threw it. It plopped harmlessly in the long grass a few yards short of the man. For a moment, the children were shocked and ashamed. They were not bad boys, nor were they angels. If the man had stood his ground, they would have melted away, pretending the incident had never happened. But the man turned and ran. He limped fast and awkwardly over the rough ground, agitated hands flapping at his sides. He looked as clumsy as a big, grounded bird. His flight was an irresistible spur to violence.

"Old devil." The boy who had flung the stone picked up another and began to run after him.

"Cut it out," yelled Wally after him. "He's got a bad foot, can't you see?" His pale face had gone crimson, his lips trembled. The children saw, amazed, that there were tears in his eyes.

"Softy," said another boy. "Cry baby."

They all began to run, shouting and waving their arms. Wally sniffed, wiping his nose on the back of his hand. Momentarily, he stood resolute, fighting his private battle. Then he stopped and picked up a bigger stone than had been thrown before and followed them, whooping louder than anyone. The man stumbled and fell sprawling. He was up in a moment, his fearful face peering over his shoulder. Wally's stone, flung hard and true, caught him on the cheek and he gave a wild yelp like a hurt dog. Hilary seized a stone and began to run. Her heart beat painfully in her throat. She threw the stone and screamed with excitement.

"I say," roared her father's voice from the gate. "Stop it at once, d'you hear?"

He ran after the boys, a ridiculous, angular figure in his neat, black suit. He was shouting. Three of the boys dived for the safety of the hedgerow and disappeared. Only Wally, more susceptible to the voice of authority than the others, waited, abashed. Charles caught up with him, seized him by the collar of his shirt and shook him violently.

"Cruel little beast," he yelled hoarsely. "You deserve a good thrashing." He cuffed the boy once or twice round the head and aimed a few ineffectual blows at his rear. Wally twisted out of his grasp and ran, howling, across the field. Charles brushed his hands together with a gesture of distaste. Cruelty of any kind aroused him to a deep and passionate anger; faced with intentional cruelty, he became a dangerous man. He walked towards Hilary, his body trembling, his eyes cold as blue pebbles.

"Did *you* have anything to do with this?" he asked grimly.

She looked up at him slowly. He saw that her eyes had a blank, dark look, almost as if she did not recognise him.

"Come on," he said, more gently. "Tell me."

"It wasn't Wally's fault," she said stoutly. "It was the others, really. And anyway, it wasn't naughty. *I* told them who he was."

"Oh. And who is he?"

She glanced at him sidelong, shuffled her feet and sighed. "Why *him*," she answered after a brief interval. "You know. The man in the newspaper. The man they're looking for."

He felt the blood beating in his forehead. "What on earth do you mean?"

Her voice was calm, almost monotonous, as if she had learned her piece by rote. "The one who took the little girl away. I saw him at the competition. I wouldn't go with him, though. But I know him. He talks to me."

She brought out these last two sentences with a kind of perky pride that dispelled his first, sharp fear. *All children tell lies*, he thought.

He said angrily, "Hilary, I hate a liar."

"But I'm *not*," she cried, suddenly as angry as he. She stamped her foot. "Peregrine knows about him, too."

"Knows what?" he asked coldly. "What you told him? What you read in the newspaper?"

She frowned. "Oh, no. I didn't tell him *that*. I mean that Peregrine knows he is the Devil."

She brought out this monstrous statement with what seemed to him a quite appalling air of innocence, looking him straight in the eye.

He said horrified, "Do you know what you're saying?"

"Of course I know what I'm saying," his daughter replied impatiently. "I know all about the Devil. But it wasn't me who knew he was the Devil *first*. It was Peregrine. He *told* me. He recognised him, you see, when we saw him taking her away." The hectic colour rose in her cheeks. "And of course he must be right. He's so good. He wouldn't tell me a fib, would he?"

Charles stared at her. There was no question of this thing being some childish nightmare that she and Peregrine had dreamed up between them. In that event, she would have trembled, wept—certainly she would not have produced the lie in this bold, bright way. "Hilary," said her school report, "has an unfortunate manner." She could never look crestfallen or properly contrite. When she felt really guilty, she looked insolent. Now, this inability to express the correct emotion was her downfall. Although she was really very much afraid, she regarded her father with a hard, triumphant stare.

He felt a complete revulsion from her. She was trying to distract his attention from the main issue by a pack of blasphemous lies. He said, wrathfully, "Hilary, did you, or did you not, throw a stone at that poor old man?"

She gazed at him wonderingly. "Yes, I did. But I've told you *why*."

Charles gave way to his righteous anger. His blue eyes grew hot with disgust, his lips trembled. To think that his child should have so little feeling for the weak and helpless! Heroically, he took some of the blame upon himself. His neglect of her must have been fearful to have led to this!

"That's all I wanted to know," he said in an ominous voice and, taking her arm, led her to a convenient tree stump at the side of the field. He sat down and, clasping her wrists, held her prisoner in front of him.

"Listen to me," he said. "That man you read about in the newspaper is in prison. So you lied to me. That is quite bad enough. But you did something much, much worse. You threw a stone at a cripple, at a poor sick man who had never done you any harm. And then tried to make me forget about it by telling me a lot of wicked lies." His voice shook with emotion. "Don't you see that this was a dreadful thing to do?"

"But he *is* the man," she cried, confused, "and he *is* the Devil."

"That's blasphemy. But I'm not going to punish you for that. Not for lying to me. I'm going to punish you for wanting to hurt someone who was poor and old and frightened." He remembered Peregrine's burnt lips and his resolve was strengthened. "I hope this will be a lesson to you will remember all your life."

She saw his intention and her eyes dilated. "No," she screamed, and tried to pull away from him.

He flung her, face downwards, across his lap. Fighting against him, arching her back, she saw, with terrible clarity, Cooper, standing at the gate and looking in their direction. With an anguished cry she clutched at her skirt. Charles did not notice Cooper. He was full of distaste for what he was about to do but he was sternly intent on justice and preventive punishment. Knowing that humiliation would make her remember the occasion more than any pain he would be willing to inflict, he deliberately raised her skirt and ripped off her knickers. He caught her flailing arms and gripped them between his knees. He beat her, with sharp, ringing slaps, until her plump behind was rosy. The sight of the red weals on her bare flesh roused in him a painful sympathy. Afraid that he might be diverted from his purpose by soft-heartedness, he continued to spank her with a heavier hand than he had intended. She hung, limp and screaming, across his knees. The birds, alarmed by her cries, rose from the trees and wheeled and called above them. When he had finished, he released her hands and pushed her off his lap. He rubbed his stinging hands against his trousers. She grovelled on the ground, choking, the saliva running out of her mouth. He was bitterly ashamed. Violence accomplished nothing and was always wrong. There was no excuse.

"Get up," he said. "Put your knickers on."

She obeyed him, fumbling with her underclothing. He averted his eyes. When she was tidy, he said wretchedly. "I've never done that before, have I? I hope you will never forget it. I hope I never have to do it again."

"I hate you," she said, between sobs, burning with shame and injustice. "I hope God will strike you dead."

"Get in the car," he said, and pointed to the gate. She turned and ran, yellow skirt blowing like a flower under the blue arc of the sky. She ran straight into Cooper, her head striking him hard in the softness of his ageing belly. He grunted and held her away from him, an amused grin on his face.

"Been a naughty girl, have you?" he said cheerily. "A bit big to have your bottom smacked, aren't you?"

He was a horrible, hateful, vulgar man. Hilary longed to die: life, in face of this disaster, was insupportable. She covered her face with her hands and wept.

"There, there," said Cooper, who was kindly natured. "It's all over now, isn't it?"

"No," she wailed in black despair. "Never. I hate him. It's not fair."

"Hush your mouth," said Cooper suddenly in quite a different voice. He flung his cigarette away and called, "It's all right, Mr. Bray. Hang on. I'm coming."

Charles could not remember clearly what had happened in the field: all that remained was the memory of an emotion that was fading like a dream on waking. In the moving car, leaning his head against the cold leather, he had a sense of unreality. He saw Cooper's back, the pale tear on Hilary's cheek, the houses, the cliffs, the sea, and felt them to be illusions that would vanish if he touched them. His limbs had become large and swollen. If he moved, he felt it would be slowly and heavily like a deep-sea diver.

The car stopped. "Here we are," said Cooper in a jolly voice. "Out you get, young lady."

Hilary stalked, her back humped like an angry cat's, into the gateway of Peebles. Cooper's anxious face appeared in Charles's line of vision. "Sure you don't want to get out too, Mr. Bray? That was a nasty turn you had, up in the field. You ought to have a good lie down."

"Take me to the shop," said Charles in an odd, slurred voice. As the car moved off, he murmured, "Poor child," and was seized with an attack of giddiness so violent that he closed his eyes. For a moment, it seemed as if all the blood cells in his body were rushing towards his throat in a mass conspiracy to choke him. Then, as he waited clutching at the soft, puffy seat, the moment passed and, he felt weak and curiously free of his body. The sky wheeled above his head, the sun made a trail like lightning across it and his spirit floated on the wind over the glittering holiday town. He sighed, his jaw hung slackly. The car passed Gorings and he saw red lobsters arranged on the fishmonger's slab like a painting. A child in a sun hat carried a bunch of flags for his sandcastle. Miss Fleery-Carpenter in white, woollen stockings and a moth-eaten fur cape, muttered to herself on the pavement and made extravagant gestures.

The car swung into the narrow, back street and stopped outside the book shop. Cooper, his left arm laid affectionately along the back of the seat, grinned at Charles. There was a sweat line on his collar and he had not shaved. Once, he would have got out and opened his passenger's door, doffing a respectful cap. But why should he, thought Charles, surprised, an old man in his sixties?

Cooper said, "You look better, Mr. Bray. More colour in your face. Been overdoing it a bit, haven't you?"

"Have to be careful, now," Charles muttered. His voice was stronger, more normal.

"None of us is getting any younger."

"No."

Cooper said, "D'you know who I took to the station this morning?"

Charles shook his head, clutching at coins in his pocket.

Cooper leaned closer. His breath was foul. "Mrs. Jenkins, poor woman. Her and her husband. They buried the little girl quiet yesterday."

"Jenkins? Oh, yes . . ." Charles bent his head. The thought was too painful, he shrank from it.

"She said there was a lovely lot of flowers. Wish I'd thought to send a nice wreath myself. It must have been a comfort, all those people thinking of them. She kept on about it all the time: it was so kind of everyone, she said. And such a lovely funeral, she looked so pretty in her coffin. I wouldn't take the fare from them although she kept on offering it and afterwards I wished I had because it made her cry. But it wasn't anything of course . . ."

Cooper was talking in a confidential voice. The flash of genuine feeling that had briefly illuminated him was gone and his expression displayed simply a kind of greedy eagerness. "Just as well it happened at the end of the Season. Bad for business. Most of us would be finding things a bit tight. Stands to reason, no one wants to bring their kids to a place where they might get their throats cut. Would you, I ask you?"

"I suppose not," said Charles carefully, edging his way out of the car. The whole business sickened him, he did not want to discuss it. "Anyway," he concluded, standing on the pavement and smiling at Cooper, "they'd be safe enough now."

He fancied that Cooper looked surprised. He took off his cap and scratched his head, then opened his mouth to speak. But Charles had had enough. He did not want to have to listen, to smile. The demands of other people clawed at his nerve ends with savage fingers, affecting him like the scrape of a nail across a blackboard. His head felt enormous: he would need all his strength to carry him down the stairs to his tiny, private room, his haven, the peace of his old school desk.

He did not reach it. Miss Hubback met him as he entered the shop. She was weeping, her delicate, absurd nose swollen to the size and colour of a plum. Her generous tears confused the issue: at first, Charles thought that it was a purely private matter that distressed her. That it was not, he understood at last after some moments of disordered conversation. She brought him the morning papers which he had not seen, sobbing her kind heart out at the sadness and uncertainty of life. The man the police had held for questioning had been released. He had been seen by an old lady to buy an ice cream for a child who had since been found to be alive and well. The police were looking for the murderer.

Miss Hubback wondered at the expression on Charles's face and also, some time afterwards, at some of the things he said, not to her but to himself. His words were vague and rambling, there seemed to be something wrong with his speech. She caught something about Hilary, there was something that she had done, or said that troubled him. He said in a soft, wondering voice, so low that she had to strain to catch the words, "She could have seen him . . . it is quite possible . . . what a terrible situation for her . . ." Then, in a stronger voice, "I have behaved abominably. . . ."

"No," cried Miss Hubback, shocked. "Never, Mr. Bray."

He looked up at her after a brief silence, his face ghastly and hollowed like a skull so that she brushed aside what he was trying to tell her and offered, alarmed, to fetch a doctor. But he shook his head and tried to smile. He was perfectly well, he insisted, a little tired, that was all. Really all. . . .

The man kept on running. It hurt him to run and he was slow: he got over the chopped ground with a curious hop and skip and looked like Worzel Gummidge. After a while, he forgot why he was running. He only knew that the fear inside him was like a pain, as real a pain as the wound on his cheek. He avoided his caravan like a frightened animal and made for the cliffs. When he reached them, he went straight down over the sides, clinging like a fly. The tide was going out and the beach was empty except for a bent figure paddling some distance away at the edge of the sea. Once on the shore, he felt safe. He smiled to himself and began to limp along the shingle. Then he looked up and saw a policeman, black against the skyline.

Panic seized him. He was frightened of policemen. He fled into the nearest cave. It was wedge-shaped and sandy with high, chalk sides closing above his head. Most of it was above high water mark because the floor was carpeted with dry seaweed and stirring with sand-flies. He went straight to the cold depth of the cave and crouched by a petrol drum that was full of rubbish from the shore. He stirred it hopefully and a stench arose, offending his nostrils. He kicked it over angrily and the mess rolled out among the seaweed. He saw maggots crawling over the breast of a long-dead gull and he gathered up the seaweed with his hands, covering the body. Then he waited, crouching on his haunches, biting his fingernails.

He heard the shingle scattering outside the cave and began to whimper softly, watching the entrance. It darkened and he put his hands across his eyes.

Someone came inside the cave. He peered between his spread fingers and saw a woman bending over the spilled petrol drum. She righted the drum and began to pick up the

contents. A smell of putrefaction filled the cave. A whirl of
flies arose. He stood up slowly and carefully and stared
curiously at her, wondering what she was doing. She was
old, he saw, as old as his grandmother. Her hair was wild
and white, she wore a pink blouse and a pair of mackintosh
trousers fastened at the waist with a silver belt. Her bare
ankles were thick and pulpy looking with a discoloured
network of veins across the bone. She was completely
absorbed in what she was doing. She filled the drum and
covered the rubbish with seaweed. Then she stood upright
and saw him.

A low, surprised grunt came from the back of her throat.
She moved backwards, her outspread hands pressed
nervously against the cold, chalk wall.

"What do you want?" she asked him in a loud, harsh
voice.

He shook his head stupidly, mouthing at her. His eyes
gleamed dully in his lean face, beneath the lank, dark
hair.

"What do you want?" she repeated. Her hand went
up to the bright brooch that fastened her blouse at the
neck. Her hand was old, covered with brown spots and
trembling. He saw that she was afraid and this upset him.
He frowned. He would not hurt her, he would never hurt
a poor, old woman who looked like his grandmother.
The brooch was pretty but he did not want it. He moved
indecisively towards her and she cringed against the wall
of the cave, her mouth drooping open. She looked very
ugly with her scalp showing through the thin strands of
hair and the loose flesh quivering over her jawbone. Her
ugliness disgusted him: her fear made him very angry.
He stretched out his long, bony hands, clenching and
unclenching the fingers, feeling their strength. As she
crouched and shook he grinned at her like a dog, knowing,

133

before he touched her, how soft and unresisting the flesh would be about her throat.

A sound diverted him. He turned, his hands loosely swinging and looked at the mouth of the cave. He saw the white sea fling back the screaming gravel. He saw, against the suddenly darkening sky, the policeman pass.

He gave a soft, singing moan and fled, hands flapping, to the back of the cave. There, he flung himself down in a heap, burying his face in the collar of his coat.

A hand touched his shoulder. He looked up in fear and saw the old woman bending over him. "What's the matter? Are you ill?" He heard, in her clear, upper-class voice, the authority that had always pursued him. He shrank from her. Sighing, she felt in the pocket of her trousers and held out a few, small coins.

"Here," she said. "Take this. Don't come back here, ever. This is *my* cave. Do you understand?"

Auntie had no illusions as to what his intentions had been towards her. Now she knew he would not harm her, she dismissed his behaviour from her mind. He could not be dangerous, she told herself, not this abject bag of bones. There was no need to mention the matter to anyone, no need to explain her own presence in the cave.

She sighed thankfully, placed the money on a flat, white stone beside him and turned away. She took her clothes from a ledge that jutted out from the side of the cave. She fastened her cloak round her neck and thrust her skirt and shoes into a large, inside pocket. She gave him a last, doubtful look and left the cave. He crawled on his belly over the stinking seaweed. He reached the petrol drum and rested there.

The policeman had returned. He heard his voice and then the old woman's. They were standing by the entrance to the cave. He could see the corner of her cloak as it blew out in the wind. He trembled and chewed at his fingers.

"No officer," she said. "I've been shrimping. I've been dressing in this cave. There is no one there."

They went away. For the moment he could not believe in his safety. He crept to the mouth of the cave. The little bay in which the cave lay hidden was empty. He was safe. Dark clouds drove across the sky like a falling curtain. He smiled and chattered to himself.

Then he grew suspicious. Why had she not given him away? There must be something in the cave she had not wanted the policeman to see, something she had hidden there. Frowning, he stared at the damp, smooth walls. Perhaps she had hidden something in the petrol drum. He laughed excitedly and flung himself upon it, churning up the rubbish. Rotten fish gleamed like jewels in the dark seaweed, their transparent bellies shining with the pale colours of the rainbow. He cut his thumb on a broken piece of glass, sucked the blood away and bound the cut with his handkerchief. One-handed, he delved deeper and came upon something wrapped in a piece of dirty sailcloth. He laid it carefully on one side. This was her treasure, he thought, smiling. She was clever to have hidden it like this. Oh, she was cunning, but not cunning enough for him. He emptied the drum without further interest and kicked it contemptuously away from him. The stench was too much for his nostrils. Grimacing with disgust, he picked up the precious bundle and left the cave. The sea air blew cleanly in his face, carrying a hard spatter of rain. He sighed happily and sat down upon a rock. Tenderly, he unwrapped the sailcloth and saw it was a shroud.

Screaming, he flung it down and ran. He went back up the cliffs with fear behind him, the soft clay slipping beneath his feet. The cold wind blew from the north, blowing away the fine weather, the last of the summer. The cliff tops were empty. There was no one to see him, flattened against the sides of the cliff, clutching at lumps of coarse, grey grass. He went the way that Hilary had gone the day before and came upon the fallen garden, sheltered in its hollow. He stayed there, out of the wind, and when the rain began to fall more heavily he crawled inside an empty water tank that lay on its side near to the broken, concrete pool. The rain thudded on the zinc sides like rifle shots but he felt safe there, enclosed and unobserved. After a little while, when the noise ceased to trouble him, he fell asleep.

On the beach near the cave, the cat that Auntie had wrapped in sailcloth lay where he had thrown it; stiff, dead eyes staring, paws folded back on its breast. The mouth was open, the lips curled back showing the dainty, savage teeth. The tide crept up the beach and took it. It bobbed in the yellow scum at the edge of the water and, for a time, took on a semblance of life. Then the sea washed it higher up the beach and it lodged between two rocks, lying on its back and snarling at death.

"It's not *fair*," said Hilary hopelessly, staring at her mother. "Nothing is ever fair." She had learned one lesson from the episode in the field and not one that Charles had intended. Once her first, dreadful humiliation had faded, she bore no malice against her father. She did not understand why he had beaten her: she simply and philosophically accepted it as a sign that life never was, and never would be, just.

"Don't be silly, dear." Sitting in the kitchen in her pretty, flowered apron, Alice shelled peas into a colander.

Hilary shucked a pod and found a fat maggot inside.

"You didn't tell me he was going away," she accused. "I don't see why I couldn't have gone too."

"Because you couldn't," snapped Alice. Her head was splitting and she felt ill-used. She had been unprepared for Hilary's abrupt return: she had expected Charles to keep her with him for the rest of the morning. How like him, she thought with mounting bitterness, to dodge his responsibilities in this fashion. None of her plans ever turned out as she intended them to do—on this occasion, even Peregrine had been difficult. He had shown no pleasure at the prospect of his holiday. He had even wept on hearing that Hilary was not to accompany him and, sitting tear-stained beside Janet in the taxi that was to take him to the station, he had threatened to be sick in the train and had refused to kiss his mother.

"You wanted to get me out of the way," screamed Hilary suddenly and flew into a rage. She cast herself on to the floor, drumming her heels and grinding her teeth. Her eyes, screwed into slits, spurted water.

"Ah," said Alice, "I thought that was the matter with you."

"Of course," said Charles aloud, "that's what's the matter with me."

He set down his glass with extreme care. Watching his reflection in the lighted mirror behind the gin and whisky bottles, he saw that his neighbour at the shining bar was regarding him suspiciously.

Turning on his stool, Charles smiled at him gravely. "Do you know," he confided, "that was my first whisky?" His skin was pearly pink, his eyes very blue and bright. "In five years," he ended, and slid gracefully off his stool.

The sea front was empty and shone with rain. Water streamed in the gutters and enclosed the houses like a curtain.

Women in summer dresses crowded into Woolworth's for shelter and trod between the counters with unregarding eyes. Beneath a driving sky, the tide ebbed across the stinking mud.

Charles leaned on the rail and gazed at the deserted beach. Rain sluiced down his neck and polished his hair like silk.

"Left behind by the tide," he said, "that's what's wrong." Nodding his head, he was filled with a great solemnity. Then, mocking himself, he smiled. He had amounted to nothing but what, in the end, did it matter? He lifted his head and walked along the front, ignoring the rain. He reached the steps that led from the promenade to the main street and ran up them like a boy.

He found himself opposite the police station. The blue lamp, the square, red-brick, white-painted frontage, cleared his mind. He remembered what he had been going to do when guilt and indecision had driven him, for the first time for years, into a public house. He remembered, quite clearly now what had happened in the field: the painted caravans, the cripple and his own daughter, in a yellow dress, throwing a stone at a murderer. He did not doubt, now, that this had been the case. It seemed to him incredible that he should ever have thought she was lying. With a deep and growing shame, he saw his criminal failure as a father and a citizen.

He stepped off the gleaming pavement and a bright pain seized him. It travelled along his left arm and pointed a dagger at his heart. He stood rigid, one arm raised as if to ward off an enemy. Slowly, the pain receded and left him weak and afraid. Colder than the rain, he felt the sweat on his forehead. Cautiously he moved his limbs and felt nothing except a slight stiffness in one arm. He sighed on a long, trembling breath. Through the fear that clouded his mind, one thought stayed constant: he must get to Hilary. His daughter was more important than the murderer: the police would get *him*, poor devil, soon enough. Hilary was his business. He had let her down badly, he must put this right between them. If he failed in everything else, he must not fail in this. He turned his back on the police station and began to walk carefully down the long, wet street.

"I want Daddy," said Hilary perversely. She had cried out the storm, her eyes peered out of swollen sacks of flesh. She scowled heavily at her mother who waited, anxious to be kind, beside her.

"Darling." Alice stretched out a loving hand and Hilary closed her lips and turned away. The rebuff was intentional and Alice knew it. She stood up and went to the door.

"Wait then," she said. "He'll be home soon." She hesitated and added, in a colder tone, "And change your dress. It'll be fit for nothing, lying on the floor."

Her eyes shut, Hilary heard the door close. She lay still, tears of real sorrow squeezing between her puffy lids. Then, getting to her feet, she took a handful of peas from the colander on the table and chewed them absently. They tasted mealy: the season was over. The kitchen was empty and silent except for a dripping tap. She felt her body surrounding her like an unfamiliar envelope. Looking down, she saw her two feet in grubby, white socks and patent shoes. This is me, she thought, my two feet, my two, silly, fat hands. Lonely, suddenly, she began to cry a little and opened the kitchen door. Climbing the stairs, the house seemed empty: she held her breath. Creeping across the landing she saw, through the half-open bedroom door, her mother's motionless back. Alice stood before her dressing-table, hands resting on the polished wood, bright head sunk forward between hunched shoulders. *She* is crying, thought Hilary, surprised, and a lump rose in her own throat. She longed for her mother to turn and see her: her pride forbade her to make the first move. Suffering and alone, she passed into the nursery where she dragged off her party dress and flung it in a yellow heap on a chair. Peregrine's white bed, already stripped, the folded blankets lumpy beneath the counterpane, mocked her from its corner. She commented in a low voice on the other signs of his absence. "His dressing-gown, gone from the door, gone his red slippers with the rabbit's head, gone his Meccano box."

She refused to cry, instead she admired her stoic face in the mirror with the painted, wooden frame. Ah, she was brave! Surrounded on all sides by savage tribes, outnumbered, she faced death heroically. "Too late the Phalarope," she murmured. This was a phrase she had heard her mother use at a tea party and it had remained with her ever since. The words seemed to Hilary mysterious and noble, in times of crisis, they comforted her soul.

Then she remembered the Devil and the magic ceased to work. Her face, in the mirror, shrank and altered; she turned away from it lest she should see his face, dim and awful, looking over her shoulder. In her vest and knickers, she climbed on to a chair and looked out of the barred window at the soaked Downs, the muddy sea. A cluster of trees immediately opposite the house made a dreadful hiding-place. Was he waiting for her there? She began to tremble, a fear greater than anything she had felt before possessed her. She felt his presence round her, she did not dare to turn her head.

Then she saw her father's head, bobbing beyond the

dripping hedge of the front garden. He stopped, opened the gate and glanced upwards at the windows of his house as he always did on coming home. Her misery, her humiliation were forgotten: she felt a warm tide of comfort and relief. He was not angry with her any more. He knew everything. He had come back.

"Daddy," she shrieked, and tumbled off her chair.

Charles knew everything—or almost everything. He even, with a leap of imagination unusual in him, understood the significance of the club foot. And yet, as he climbed the hill, he found it difficult to concentrate on Hilary. His mind, while acknowledging the seriousness of the situation, kept slipping away from it and wandering along side alleys. He measured Hilary's Devil against his own childhood fears. They had not been many: his parents had been sensitive and kindly people who had never forced him, while he showed the slightest unwillingness, to swim or to ride a bicycle. They had provided a night light in his nursery to shut out the dark which he did not fear. Any admitted terror would have been dispelled with kindness and understanding. It had not been their fault that he could not speak of the one thing that had made the winter evenings terrible.

A black puma crouched above the well of the stairs waiting to pounce upon him. He knew the look of the puma intimately. It had a sleek, shining fur like his mother's moleskin coat, one large, golden eye and long, raking claws like marlin spikes. It was not there when he was in the bathroom or the lavatory. It did not threaten him until he was below, in the hall. Even then, he was safe until he passed beneath the dark well which lay between the foot of the stairs and the drawing-room and safety. Sometimes he could not face the danger. He would stand, shivering, at the bottom of the stairs, cold with fear, waiting for the drawing-room door to open and a grown-up to appear.

He told no one. He bore his fear alone. Looking back, it seemed to him that his silence on the matter meant, not that he was brave, but that his fear was too great to be told. Puffing slightly, he turned in at his gate. He saw his daughter pressed against the bars of the nursery window and would have waved to her if he had had the strength. As he opened the front door, fumbling a little with the familiar lock, he felt a warning tremor in his arm. He became conscious of his heart, labouring like an engine in too high a gear.

He remembered, then, that he *had* told someone about the puma. He had cried out to his grandmother one day when he was sick and she was sitting by his bed making paper dolls to amuse him. She had not ridiculed him: the puma was too real to be destroyed by laughter. She had said just the right thing. If only, he thought, I could remember what she said, I would know what to say to Hilary.

He saw his daughter standing at the top of the stairs. He saw her brilliant hair, her plump, freckled legs. Her plain, clever face seemed suddenly unbearably pathetic. He knew that he loved her dearly. He thought that she cried out to him. "Wait," he said, "I'm coming." The stairs were steeper than he expected them to be. The pain took him, not with fear but rather with surprise, so that the expression on his face, as he fell, was one of extraordinary astonishment.

He spoke once before he became completely unconscious. Alice, who had come in response to Hilary's frightened cry thought he said—though it seemed ridiculous— "Who's afraid of an old puma?" He lay still. The green light from the stained glass of the landing window, playing on his extreme pallor, gave his skin a luminous, shining look. At first, she thought he was dead, but when she and Mrs. Peacock had lifted his heavy body on to the bed, they found that a faint breath, lingering in his shattered body, misted the small mirror they held to his lips.

Chapter Seven

Charles was ill, seriously so. He did not know it. He knew nothing. He lay mindless, a stiff, heavy hulk upon a Dunlopillo mattress beneath an eiderdown of shell pink silk. The room, for ten years his shared, matrimonial bedroom, reflected not his, but Alice's taste. He had never liked the frills and flounces, the lamps draped in pleated silk, the peach-tinted mirrors and now their robust femininity triumphed over his death-bed. He was to die as he had lived, unable to impress himself upon his surroundings.

Alice moved between the sickroom and the kitchen, dry-eyed and proud. Her face was impassive and rejected pity. She accepted the fact that Charles was dying and calmly planned for the future. They had been living, beyond their income, on the little capital that Charles's mother had left him. That money was almost gone and the bookshop had never been successful. With luck, she could sell out to the new chain-store in the High Street that sold birthday cards and stationery as well as books and ran a twopenny library.

Coldly, she looked beyond death to a modified poverty and did not fear it. Instead, a kind of exhilaration took possession of her. She was at her best in just this sort of practical disaster. At last her real talents, her tenacity, her shrewdness, her courage, could be put to some real use. She could sell the house or take in paying guests. Four spare rooms could be arranged if she and the children moved up to the unused attic floor. Ten guineas a week in summer, a little less for the right kind of permanent resident. Five mouths to feed. The children's education to pay for—whatever happened, *they* must not suffer. Frowning, she sat by her husband's side and worked out sums on a piece of paper.

Hilary sat in a corner of the kitchen, hunched on a wicker chair. She held the kitten in her lap. Its soft paws puddled against her thigh, the flat head nuzzled into her warm hand. Her freckled face was closed and secret: behind it, demons raged. Children can feel guilt as deeply as adults and Hilary was no exception. She had not been told her father was dying but she knew the truth. Had she not wished God to strike him dead? She was a murderer—and not for the first time.

Last summer she had played on the beach with a boy called Cyril who had had an operation on his head. He was a big boy, nearly fourteen, but he played with the little ones because he was slow and stumbling and childish. They had been playing hide-and-seek. He had followed her into one of the caves and tried to kiss her. Frightened, because he was big and had a white, stupid face, she had pushed him away and he fell, striking his head on a stone. She had run out of the cave into the sun and pretended that she did not know where he was. Her relief, when he eventually rejoined the other children, had been boundless. Then, a week later, Alice had told her that Cyril was dead. The boy had died of a tumour on the brain: a final operation had been too late to save him. Hilary, however, did not know this and believed his death to be the direct result of his fall in the cave. She told no one, she suffered her dreadful knowledge in silence. Time had softened her wretchedness but she had never forgotten the incident. Now it returned to her with redoubled force. She had killed her father as certainly as she had killed Cyril. She was wicked beyond redemption.

Mrs. Peacock, seeing her solemn little figure, retired into the outside lavatory and sobbed loudly and gloriously. Poor Mr. Bray; his poor, fatherless children. Her tears were the tears she shed at christenings and funerals alike: she wept for the beautiful sadness of life. After a little, she dried her eyes and, coming back into the kitchen, gave Hilary a bar of chocolate.

Alice, noticing the child, so still and quiet, felt a stab of pity. Had she neglected her? She should have seen that she had something to keep her busy.

She said, in a bracing voice, "Darling, would you go on an errand for us? We've run out of tea."

The child's quick, recoiling movement, the slight enlargement of her pupils, went unnoticed.

"It's dark," Hilary said and looked at the limitless blackness behind the uncurtained window.

"Nonsense, dear. Not really dark, not yet. Not outside."

She took Hilary's coat from the peg behind the kitchen door, slipped it over the unresisting arms, buttoned it across her chest.

"It's raining," said Hilary helplessly, her eyes wide and strained.

Alice laughed at her. "Why, silly one, it stopped an hour ago. You'd like to help us, wouldn't you?"

Hilary nodded. Something was going to happen to her and she was powerless to stop it. It was like a dream. She felt the roughness of her tweed coat against the back of her knees, the cold coins in her hand. Her mother's face, Mrs. Peacock's, floated above her smiling false smiles, cut off from her as by a wall of glass. Then she was in the long hall, smelling of polish, her mother's hand on her shoulders. Alice opened the front door on to the grey dusk and the wild wind.

"Look, a lovely evening. It'll do you the world of good. Get some air into your lungs. Run."

At the gate, Hilary turned. For a moment, her mother stood at the door, the lovely light streamed safely along the gravel path. Then the door closed and she was alone. The wet hedge brushed her cheek. She began to run, her feet echoing against the walls of the houses, looking straight in front of her. On her right, the Downs stretched to the cliff edge. She gave them one fearful glance and saw the dark tree clumps, the pale metalled paths, the silver grass. There was a pain in her chest as sharp as a needle. Puffing, she slowed down, clasping her side. A man was coming towards her, bent against the hill and the wind. She stopped, not daring to move, her doubled fist crushed against her mouth. Her wild eyes sought the houses, the nearest one was set far back behind dripping laurels and the windows were dark. Anyway, he would reach her before she had time to press the bell. He was very close now, and she whimpered a little.

He was beside her. He had passed. She held her breath. Then he stopped, turned. She felt faint and leaned against the hedge. She heard his voice, a gentle, old man's voice. "I say, is anything the matter?"

She moaned and, suddenly released, ran from the kind question, across the road and on to the grey Downs. The wet grass squeaked beneath her rubber soles. From the dark trees, blackness stretched out long fingers to snare her. Above her sobbing heart, she heard the sound of the sea; at her feet, the grass sloped steeply away to the lighted town. She caught her breath. She could go down to the town and come back to the shop on the bus. She had enough money for the fare as well as for the tea. She stumbled on to one of the tarmac paths that criss-crossed the Downs. It flickered whitely before her, leading sharply downwards. She followed it, running faster and faster until her legs were out of control and she slipped, falling sideways, her wide-flung hands grazing on a heap of stones. She cried a little with the shock and scrambled to her feet. A little below her, at the side of the path, there was a high, tangled patch of blackberry bushes. As she watched, a shadow moved beside it.

She gave a short, strangled cry and left the path, heading sideways across the grass. The wind tore at her coat, The Way was slightly uphill now and her tired, fat legs ached with effort. Then, like a miracle, she saw the small, bright shop at the end of The Way.

She reached the road. A car caught her small figure in its sweeping headlights and the driver swore, wrenching at the wheel. Safe beside the lighted window of the shop, she turned and looked back at the Downs. A patch of darkness moved, stopped and moved again.

All afternoon, the man had hidden in the tank in the fallen garden. He was safe there, he could not be seen from the cliff or from the beach. He hid without really knowing why he was hiding. Somewhere in the depths of his mind, there was a faint memory of guilt. His mother's voice: just you wait. He had run from her and hidden in the basement of a bombed house, the siren had wailed like a cat on the tiles and thump, thump, thump, the bombs had fallen, killing the family in the baker's shop at the corner of the street, killing his mother as she came out of the pub.

He stirred, became aware of the hunger crawling like

148

beetles in his stomach. He remembered his bird. He had
not fed it last night or this morning. He felt for the new
packet of bird seed in the pocket of his coat. He had
bought it when he had finished work. He had been going to
feed the bird when the child had pointed at him in the field.

Remembering this, the sweat stood out on his thin face.
He had been pointed at before. *"That's the boy, Mummy,
that's him." He had done nothing, only asked for a kiss because
she had pretty hair, yellow hair, soft as cotton wool, and she had
gone away screaming. The screaming had angered him and he had
followed her, trapping her against a wall. He was little and lame
and she was strong. She had hit out at him, raking sharp, dirty nails
down his face. He had run away, crying, and then they came after
him, the angry women, with hating faces and flailing arms. Dirty
beast, dirty beast.*

He whimpered, huddled in his hiding-place. He must
get out and feed his poor bird. It was getting dark, he would
be safe soon. He could crawl along the hedges in safety and
darkness.

The rain had stopped, there was no more iron hammering
on the zinc roof above him. He crept cautiously out of the
tank, cramped and aching, and looked anxiously up at the
tossing sky. He saw the last yellow light of day binding
the edges of a torn cloud.

When he reached the field, there were lights in the
windows of the caravans. As he passed, a chained dog barked
sharply and he cowered low to the ground. He heard the
ordinary everyday sounds of the caravan site: the screaming
curses of a matrimonial quarrel, Radio Luxemburg turned
on loud, the sad cry of a neglected child.

He pushed open the door of his home. Johnny, Johnny,
he called softly and stumbled against the table. His hand
groped for the candle, the frail light flickered and threw
his monstrous shadow on the dirty wall.

Johnny, he said smiling, and the bird lay on its back in the sandy tray, the helpless legs curled stiffly upwards. He touched it and it was as hard as a stuffed bird and cold.

He could not believe it was dead. He called its name and prodded it with his finger until it rolled on its side. The little eyes were covered with a faint veil, like the layer of dust on polished wood. He picked it up and held it tenderly against his cold cheek. His face darkened suddenly and he threw it away from him in disgust. Dead, he said, dead, and, staggering to the open door, retched on the ground.

A slow and terrible anger filled him. Johnny would not be dead if the red-haired child had not shouted at him. He would not have run away, he would have been able to feed his bird and it would have sung its pretty song.

He left his caravan and made his sure way through the gathering dusk, towards the Downs.

"He's dying," said Alice, in Auntie's room. She had come in suddenly and found the old woman kneeling before the open playbox. Alice saw the sea-shore rubbish, the childish treasure. So that's where she goes in the afternoons, she thought, that's her secret. The filthy old woman! And then, with fear, will *I* come to this in the end?

"You should have knocked." Auntie slammed down the lid and looked up indignantly, her eyes dead as gutted candle ends.

"Fat lot of good that would have been," Alice muttered and thought: she's afraid of me; I've found out her nasty little game and she's afraid. She doesn't care about anything else.

"I said, he's dying," she repeated harshly, "dying. That's important. Not this." She kicked the side of the playbox with her toe.

Auntie watched her anxiously for a moment for signs of disgust. Then, "No, it isn't important," she said, suddenly smiling and then hiding the smile. She got up slowly, placing her massive body between Alice and the playbox. "Is there no hope?" she asked.

"None. He'd been drinking. I smelt his breath. He wasn't supposed to drink." She went on wildly, her composure vanishing. "He *knew* he shouldn't drink. He had no right to do it. Leaving us like this, without any money. So upright, you'd think, such a responsible man. That was the front he showed, wasn't it? He had to be generous, he couldn't bear to seem poor. He had to act grandly, like a gentleman. Such airs—and he leaves us paupers. There won't be a penny," she exaggerated.

"You mustn't talk like this," cried Auntie, shocked. "Not now."

"It's all right for *you*," said Alice rudely. "You've got plenty of money. You haven't anything to worry about."

Her retort lacked fire. She was shamed by her outburst as people are always shamed by their own natural behaviour.

"Is that what you thought?" Auntie's old voice was incredulous. "Is that what he told you?"

"Not exactly. But he didn't contradict me when I said . . ." Alice reddened uncomfortably. "You mean it isn't true?"

"I haven't a penny," said the old woman. There was silence. The heavy clock ticked the seconds away. Auntie stood still and proud. "I'll leave, of course, as soon as I can make arrangements."

"Nonsense, you'll do no such thing. What sort of a bitch do you think I am?" Alice was moved but she was incapable of expressing her feeling gracefully. "You'll stay. I want you to. *My* kind don't get rid of their old people. It's only the rich who shut them up in nursing homes. *We* can't afford to."

"It's good of you," said Auntie, stiffly. Her mouth was shaking. Alice saw this with appalled pity.

"You poor old thing," she said awkwardly and ran from the room. She met Mrs. Peacock looking for her on the landing. There was no need for words. Alice went straight to her husband's bedside.

"Charles?"

His face looked defenceless and much younger. The skin on his flat cheekbones was youthfully pink. The soldierly moustache looked absurd above the kind, weak mouth. She saw a slit of light beneath his lids. "Darling," she said, with genuine love, pressing his hand, and the light was gone. She waited, trembling. Surely something stronger, more dramatic, must happen when life went out of the body? Had it happened? What had gone, if so, and what remained? She took the pocket mirror from her handbag and held it before his lips. She thought it misted slightly and then she knew she was wrong. Awed, though she had seen her mother die, she crossed his hands on his breast.

"God bless you," she said, and it came to her with sudden pain that she did not believe in God. "Poor Charles," she said his epitaph, and turning saw Mrs. Peacock at the door of the room.

"She's not back," Mrs. Peacock said. "She's been gone twenty minutes. She should have been back by now."

For a moment, Alice did not know what she was talking about. Then she said, "She's dawdling, the naughty girl." She burst into wild, shaking tears, the first she had shed. "It's over," she cried. "He's gone."

The shop was warm and bright. It sold groceries and sweets and ice cream although it had once been a draper's shop and along one wall there were still a number of fitted drawers labelled, *vests, night-caps* and, curiously, *infant's bods.*

The woman behind the counter was plump and pale. She wore a plastic collar round her neck for she had slipped a disc. This appliance fascinated Hilary: she could not take her eyes from it.

"Half a pound of tea, dear," The woman slapped two oblong packets on the counter. Hilary held out her scratched hand with the money and the woman said, "Goodness me, what have you done? Fallen over in the dark?" She looked at Hilary more closely. "Does it hurt, dearie?"

The kind, sympathetic tone brought tears to Hilary's eyes. She nodded silently.

"Well, never mind. Your mummy will bathe it when you get home, I'm sure."

"Give her something to make it better, Captain," said a woman who appeared from a curtained doorway at the back of the shop.

Hilary wondered, as always, at this curious address and stared at the newcomer who wore what appeared to be a faded, girl guide's uniform. She was about fifty, as thin as a child and with a scraggy neck like a tortoise's. A heavy, leather belt, dangling whistles and scouting knives, hung round her meagre hips.

"Shall I? I wonder, now . . ." Captain gave Hilary a bright, meaningful smile. Hilary regarded her stupidly and the thin woman leaned over the counter and said in a clear, loud voice as if she were speaking to a deaf person, "Sweeties? Don't tell me you don't like sweeties, dearie?"

To Hilary their faces, one so thin and grey, one fat and the colour of lard, seemed to flicker and recede. Boiled sweets rattled on the scales, a small paper-bag was pressed into her free hand.

"Thank you," she whispered and lingered. The darkness pressed about the little shop, ominous as thunder. Glances passed between the two women.

"Does her mother know she's out, d'you think, Captain?" said the old girl guide.

"Does your mother know you're out?" repeated the fat woman in a low, serious voice, not smiling now.

"She sent me," said Hilary in a faint voice.

The women looked at each other again. Hilary heard their voices distantly like the whisper of talk from another station when the wireless was on.

"Not right, d'you think? Not in the dark. Not now. Shall I go home with her, Captain?" said the thin one. Hilary saw them clearly now, nodding and smiling. She saw the leather belt and the sharp knives. The thin woman's eyes were queer: one was blue and the other a green colour that changed under the light. Hilary knew the women well: she had spent her Saturday money at their little shop since she had been able to toddle. But now they seemed quite unfamiliar and strange. The odd-coloured eyes, the thin face, the eccentric costume frightened her. Hilary said, "I'm all right, really. Thank you. I *like* the dark."

Their faces seemed to alter, to swell and move towards her. Hilary flung herself against the door that tinkled as she opened it. The picture postcards, hung on tapes on the inside of the door, rustled in the wind. As she went, she banged into a tiny figure.

"Wretched child," said a muttering, venomous voice. Hilary was gone and the little creature went into the shop and banged the door behind her. "I hate children," said Miss Fleery-Carpenter, clutching her wolf fur round her skinny neck.

The darkness outside was complete. Pale lamps splashed islands of safety along the pavement. She had only to run now, and she would be safe, run and no one would see her in the dark. Clasping her sweets and the soft packets of tea, she reached the first lamp and thought: under the light, he can see my hair. She crossed the road. Here there were no lamps, only the grass verge at the edge of the Downs. She splashed her feet in the puddled gutter. Then she heard the footsteps. They followed her, matching their pace to hers, footsteps that were not quite even, one step heavier than the other so that each second step seemed only an echo of the first. She began to run, the cold rain-water splashing on her bare legs but running, she could not hear the footsteps and that frightened her. So she walked as fast as she could, not daring to look round, hearing the footsteps gain upon her, slowly, slowly, counting the lamp-posts on the other side of the road. She saw, in her mind, the man behind her; his long coat blacker than the surrounding night; his terrible face, white as bone. She did not cry, she was beyond tears now. Nothing could be worse than not knowing, she thought and suddenly turned defiantly to face him. She did not see him. She saw only the long, wide road, the stirring trees, the yellow, puddled light from the lamp-posts and the thin woman from the shop whirring slowly towards her on a bicycle. She saw the spindly legs, bare to the thighs beneath the short guide dress, the kind, evil face bent towards her.

"You forgot your change." The words seemed to hold some dreadful, hidden purpose. Hilary thought: *He* can take any shape, he can look how he likes. She ran with wild fear behind her, reached the last lamp-post, reached, hurling herself against the gate, scattering the gravel, her house. Pounding on the door, the brass knocker echoing in the street, she heard voices calling her on the wind, Hilary, Hilary. The door opened and she fell forward into the hall, saved by Mrs. Peacock's hand. A grey streak, a phantom, fled past them into the night.

"The cat, the cat's out." Mrs. Peacock stood at the open door and peered out into the dreadful dark.

"Shut the door." Hilary clutched at the rough stuff of her apron.

"It'll get run over." Mrs. Peacock spoke reproachfully, stepped out into the porch.

"Shut the door, shut the door," Hilary shrieked at the top of her lungs, clapping her hands over her ears.

"Hush," said Mrs. Peacock. "What a dreadful noise. Aren't you ashamed to make a noise like that? Your poor Daddy. . . ." She shut the door and glanced uneasily at the stairs, putting her finger to her lips.

"I want Mummy," said Hilary in a lower tone. She had gone very white, the freckles stood out on her skin like stones.

Mrs. Peacock bent and wiped Hilary's running nose with the corner of her apron. "Not now, lovey. She's busy." She took the child's cold hand and led her into the kitchen. "Where have you been all this time, that's what I'd like to know. Worrying us all. Now you stay with me for a while. I tell you what—we'll make a gingerbread man. There's a bit of dough left over in the larder and I'll find you some currants for eyes. You can light the oven all by yourself."

The mixture of scolding and kindness bewildered Hilary. She stamped her foot. "No, *no*." The angry colour came back into her face.

Mrs. Peacock sniffed. "*Someone's* in a naughty temper, aren't they? You'll stay here as you're told, my girl, and no nonsense. Your Mummy's busy."

"Daddy, then," said Hilary, forgetting, and pouting her lips.

"He's very ill," said Mrs. Peacock in solemn tones. Her heart softened as she thought of the child's dreadful loss. She placed thin, loving arms about the small body. "What's the matter? Let's see if we can make it better?"

"It was dark," said Hilary in a tiny voice. "The dark. And *he* was there, the Devil. I know he was. He takes little girls away. He was waiting for me."

She looked hopefully into the small, owlish face. She saw blankness and incomprehension. She saw the thin lips tighten impatiently. "Oh, let me *go*," she said, wriggling, and pushed hard at the flat chest.

She was big and strong for her age and the sudden movement took Mrs. Peacock by surprise. The woman stepped backwards and jarred her hip-bone on the sharp corner of the kitchen table.

"Well, *I* don't know," said Mrs. Peacock crossly. "What a silly story." Her hip was extraordinarily painful and her eyes watered. She continued spitefully, "I don't know what your mother would say, I'm sure. I would have thought a little girl would have behaved better than this with her poor Daddy so ill."

"He's dead, isn't he," stated Hilary calmly. She saw nothing wrong in mentioning this fact but her disinterested tone shocked Mrs. Peacock deeply.

"Don't you *care*?" she asked, drawing a long breath and glaring at the child.

"No," said Hilary in a stony voice and burst into tears.

"I don't know what to do with her," said Mrs. Peacock. "It's a terrible thing to say of a little child, but she has no heart."

Auntie looked at the sullen child, huddled in the basketwork chair beside the stove. She had been sitting there, quite still, for the last hour. The doctor had been and gone, cups of tea had been made and drunk: she had not said a word. Her bright hair shone against the dark quilting of the chair, beneath it, her face seemed wan and dead as if the life had been sucked out of it.

"She's very pale," Auntie said.

"It's her hair. All her blood goes into her hair."

"Does she *know*?" asked Auntie in a whisper.

Mrs. Peacock rattled the cups and saucers in the sink. "Oh, she knows, all right. Quick as a monkey, that one. But that's not the trouble, believe it or not. Something frightened her in the dark."

"Hilary, come to Auntie. Come and tell me what's wrong."

Impressed by her stillness, her silence, the old woman went to her and touched her gently on the arm. Hilary looked up at her and shook her head stubbornly.

"Darling," said Auntie and bent, creaking, to touch the flaming hair.

The child's reaction was violent. She flung herself out of the chair and across the room. Back pressed against the tiled, kitchen wall, she screamed at her great-aunt. "You're no good, no *good*. You're deaf. You can't hear a word. I hate you."

"Little wretch," said Mrs. Peacock and moved angrily towards the child, her hand upraised. Auntie barred her way.

"Can't you see she's upset?" she said in ringing tones. "The best thing you can do is to fetch her mother."

"Won't he come back next week?" asked Hilary patiently. Her mother's account of what had happened to her father had confused her own, perfectly clear sense of the finality of death. It seemed, now, that he had simply departed on a journey.

"No, darling." Alice's eyes brimmed with tears at this simple innocence. "He won't come back ever again. He's gone to heaven."

"To be with God and Jesus?"

"I suppose so." Alice's voice was uncertain and Hilary looked at her shrewdly. "Don't you *know*?"

"Not, really, my precious," said Alice tenderly and took her daughter in her arms. She had no wish to impose upon her children a religion in which she could not, herself, believe. It would have seemed to her a terrible hypocrisy.

"Has he gone to hell, then?" inquired Hilary, surprised.

"Of course not." In spite of her rationalist beliefs, Alice was emotional in her strong denial. "There is no such place."

"But there is, it says so," insisted Hilary. "It says so in the Bible. 'The wicked shall be cast into everlasting fire'," she quoted with relish. Then her face contracted violently. "Besides, I've *seen* the Devil," she cried and clung to her mother.

She could not be comforted. Between outbursts of sobbing, in stumbling, incoherent phrases, she produced her fantastic story. It would have convinced no one. Truth was lost in terror, reality converted into a fairy tale. Over-wrought, poor child, thought Alice as she brought her hot milk and tucked her up in bed. The dark had frightened her, that was all, she should never have let her go out in the dark. Perhaps there had been a man— that sort of occurence was all too common. In the emotional atmosphere of her father's death and following upon the murder, such a happening would have been certain to stimulate her imagination.

She went to the window to draw the curtains, remembering, uneasily, that she had always considered Hilary an exceptionally unimaginative child. She stood, doubtful, staring at her pale reflection in the black pane. The wild night enclosed the house; above the sound of the wind, she heard the front gate bang.

"It's only Janet," she said, to comfort herself, and turning, saw the child's eyes watching her from the bed.

"I'll leave the light on, shall I?" she said.

Janet sat in the kitchen, drinking a cup of tea. Listening to her distraught sobbing, murmuring the right words at the right time, Alice was conscious of great weariness. Everything depends on me, she thought, aggrieved. The knowledge of her lonely responsibility obscured other people's sorrow.

"If only I'd been here," moaned Janet for the tenth time.

"There was nothing you could have done," said Alice, quite sharply, and poured herself another cup of tea.

"He looks so *peaceful*."

Alice reminded herself that even the most outworn of platitudes can express genuine feeling.

"I'm an orphan," announced Janet dolefully and regarded her stepmother with round, sad eyes. Her tears emphasised her youth, her skin was soft and damp and shone under the harsh kitchen light.

"At least it has happened gradually," said Alice in a bracing tone.

Janet sighed. "What am I going to do now?" she asked faintly.

"Get a job like everyone else," said Alice briskly.

Janet blushed. "When we got to Victoria, I telephoned Sheila. She was at school with me. I thought I might get a job in London and share her flat." Her expression became more animated.

"That seems an excellent idea," said Alice idly.

"Of course I couldn't *now*." Janet spoke with heavy reproach. Her face expressed resigned martyrdom.

"I don't see why not, if you want to," said Alice cheerfully. She felt a certain lightening of the heart at the thought of Janet's departure. "After all, you have to think of yourself."

"Would it be all right, really?" Her obvious relief was galling and Alice replied shortly, "Of course. I've already said so."

"Now you're angry with me," said Janet in a hurt voice and her face clouded.

"No, *no*." Alice rose from the table. "We'll discuss it to-morrow. We can't sit here all night."

She collected the tea cups and piled them in the sink. Together she and Janet saw that the doors were locked, turned out the lights. At some point they became aware that they were two women performing a man's accustomed function and their hearts faltered.

They looked down at the dead man. He looked insignificant and empty, a sack of dry bones. Alice thought: I have been married to you for ten years, you are the father of my children. Her heart remained dry and cold.

"Maggots crawling out of his eyes," whispered Janet and put her hands before her face.

"Not if he's cremated," said Alice perversely. She longed to shock the girl. "I knew a farmer in Wales," she said. "When he died, it was the middle of winter and the ground was too hard to bury him. So they kept him in the kitchen, lying on a settle in front of the fire. They rubbed salt in him to stop the smell. I don't know whether it was successful or not."

"How dreadful," said Janet automatically. She was neither amused nor shocked. She glanced at Alice, her hands twisting awkwardly together. "Shouldn't we . . ."

"Pray for him, if you want to," said Alice.

Janet coloured deeply. She blushes like a spinster lady, thought Alice, all over her body. "I don't know . . . I just thought. . . . Do you believe in it?" she asked. Her dark eyes entreated Alice.

"In prayer?"

"No." She's embarrassed, thought Alice, as if she'd been caught in a street accident without her knickers on. "In God," the girl finished, unhappily.

Alice could bear no more. Her body ached as if she had been beaten with rods. She did not mean to be unkind but she longed for the cool whiteness of the spare room bed.

"I don't believe in God," she said loudly, finishing the matter.

There was a sound outside the bedroom door and they both turned and stared. Then Alice moved swiftly but when she opened the door, the landing was empty. In the nursery, Hilary lay face downwards in her bed, breathing steadily.

"It must have been the cat," said Alice, and turned out the light.

When Janet and her mother had been to the bathroom, when their doors were safely closed for the night, Hilary slid from her room and went into her father's room. There was no light in the room but she could see the bed and the hump of his body beneath the bedclothes by the light of the street lamp in the road outside.

She did not dare go near the bed. She said, "Daddy." in a low, fearful whisper, and remained, shivering, by the door. She did not expect him to answer. She was acting a part and was aware of this herself. She did not move until the clock in the hall struck the hour with a low, theatrical boom. Then she fled from the room, back to the nursery where she stood at the window, parting the curtains and peering out into the dark.

She did not cry. She stood, tearless and still. There was nobody to help her, not even God. No Jesus to keep you safe till morning light. It was a story for babies like Father Christmas. A dream that fell to pieces when you were old enough and when that happened, only the Devil was left, waiting for you in the ruins, biting his nails and dragging his cloven hoof.

After a little, she ceased to be afraid and began to luxuriate in the drama of her lonely position. She turned on the light and stared at herself in the looking-glass, assuming an expression of suffering nobility. Then she yawned heavily, turned out the light and lay on Peregrine's bed, dragging the rough blankets over her. This was where his head went. His feet came higher up than hers because he was smaller; she curled her body slightly so that she could fit into his shape. If she lay quite still, she could almost feel the hollow his body made in the mattress, she could imagine that she *was* Peregrine. She closed her eyes and fell asleep swiftly and healthily.

Chapter Eight

Hilary was playing in the garden with Wally. Mrs. Peacock had brought him to work with her because he was wearing his new school clothes. The evening before, he had been caught robbing an orchard by an angry market gardener and although he had successfully made his escape, he had been badly frightened and fallen into a flooded ditch. When he returned home, late and soaked to the skin, Mrs. Peacock had not been angry about the robbery. She knew that Wally was not a delinquent but had merely been experimenting to see what he could get away with. She was, however, very angry about his clothes which could not be dried overnight in the caravan. There was no alternative but to put him in his best clothes and, knowing that he would find it impossible while engaged upon his usual activities to keep them clean, she decided to keep him under her eye.

At first, he was surly with Hilary. He could not be friendly with her because she reflected, too painfully, his own, crippling disadvantages. Like him, she was too fat and too clever: this similarity which should have formed a bond between them, established her in Wally's mind as someone to be avoided.

Hilary was still too young to dislike Wally for this reason. Although she often wondered, with secret terror, why she had no friends, she did not know she was clever and her feelings for Wally were so blinding that she did not see him as fat.

Once they were alone and unobserved, her loving admiration disarmed Wally entirely. He even indulged her by playing Hide and Seek, a game which he would normally have considered beneath his dignity. When they were puffed, they sat on the steps of the wooden summer house at the bottom of the garden and ate squashed-fly biscuits—a term hastily invented by Wally to discourage Hilary from eating the currants of which he was extravagantly fond. She picked them carefully out of the biscuits and handed them to him.

"I'm going to the Fun Fair this afternoon," he said grandly. "It's the last day. And it's *my* last day, too. I'm going to school to-morrow. To my new school." He said this proudly but Hilary was unaware of the significance of his achievement and merely said, "I wish I could go to the Fun Fair," and sighed.

"I could've gone to the pictures. My Mum gave me five shillings." He plunged his hands deep into his pockets, rattled the coins and scratched himself.

"Would you take me?" she said ingratiatingly. "I've got some money in my Pig."

He shook his head. "Your Mum wouldn't let you go. Not now your father's dead. Have you seen him?" he asked curiously.

"I looked last night. But it just looked as if he was asleep. I didn't go close," she admitted honestly.

"I saw a dead man once. In the street. He was run over."

"Was he bloody?"

"No," he said, his voice tinged with regret. "He was sort of yellow. His head was hanging off the edge of the pavement. He looked all loose, like a Guy Fawkes."

"It must be funny to be dead," said Hilary in a speculative tone. "I suppose we were dead before we were born."

This idea surprised Wally. He picked his nose reflectively.

"I dunno. I suppose we can't have been really. I mean we weren't there, were we?"

"You aren't when you're dead. You rot away."

"Yes, but it's different."

"You go to heaven."

"That's what they *say*," said Wally significantly. They both stared in front of them for a short space, absorbed in this difficult problem. Finally Hilary said, "I'm sorry Daddy was horrid to you yesterday. It was all my fault."

"It wasn't nothing." Wally was appalled that she should have mentioned the matter. He rose from the step, whistling casually and began to kick at the rotten wood of the summer house.

Hilary felt his coldness towards her and said ingratiatingly, "He spanked *me*. On my bare skin."

Wally was comforted by this admission. "Did you have any marks?"

"I don't know. I couldn't see. I expect I was black and blue."

"Let's see."

Hilary drew away from him. "No. It's rude," she said priggishly.

Wally flushed to the roots of his hair. "Soppy," he shouted angrily.

"I'm *not*." Wally began to walk away and she ran after him pleadingly. "I'll let you if you like."

"Think I *want* to?" he sneered. "I bet it isn't worth seeing. My Dad once went for me with a belt. It had a buckle on the end and it cut me right open. The people next door sent for the Cruelties. There was an awful row."

"Did he go to prison? Your father, I mean."

"Nope. It was the first time. I'd pinched some apples off a barrer and he was learning me. I deserved it, all right," he ended righteously.

"Well, I didn't," Hilary burst out indignantly. "I hadn't stolen anything. I only threw one stone. And after all, it was the Devil. It wasn't wrong to throw stones at *him*."

Wally saw her earnest expression and his face became serious. "See here, kid," he said in a suddenly assumed American accent, "that wasn't the Devil, you might as well get it straight. It was only Dotty Jim. He lives in a caravan in our field. He's just ordinary, like everyone else, only a bit soft in the head. He sweeps the roads."

"Peregrine says he's the Devil," she cried, and he laughed at her.

"I shouldn't listen to *him*. He's only a little kid. Little kids get funny ideas sometimes."

She frowned crossly and stuck out her lower lip. "He said you could tell he was the Devil because he's got a cloven hoof, so there." She glared at him and he smiled in a superior manner.

"That's his club foot." He saw that she did not understand and began to explain to her with an air of condescension. "You see, some people are born sort of wrong."

"Have you *seen* his foot?" she broke in triumphantly.

"No . . ." he conceded, "but . . ."

"Then you can't *know*, can you?" Drunk with the power of her own logic, she turned a somersault in the wet grass.

"Seeing isn't always believing," he said loftily. She saw his sulky look and jumped hastily to her feet.

"Anyway, he's a bad, horrible man," she temporised.

"Oh, don't be daft." Bored and irritated, he turned away from her, wriggling inside his clothes and jerking his hips. She caught his arm. "He *is*. He was in the paper. He's the man who took the little girl away."

"What d'you mean? The one who done her in?" His

167

expression was blank and incredulous; behind it, he was dismayed. Hilary pushed her round, obstinate face close to his.

"He was sitting next to us at Uncle Jack's. Afterwards he talked to the little girl on the beach and they went away and after that I saw her picture in the paper."

Wally was too well acquainted with the boastful lie not to recognise the truth when he heard it. He also knew enough about the world to know that Dotty Jim might easily be that kind of murderer. His heart shrank inside him. His maturity dropped away and he looked, suddenly, small and frightened.

"Have you *told* anyone?" he asked in a hoarse voice.

Hilary saw the change in him with dismay. "They didn't believe me," she said helplessly.

"Grown-ups." The scorn in his voice lacked conviction. He began to bluster. "You can't 'ave told them proper. You should have told someone important, like a policeman."

"Oo, I daren't."

"Well, you got to do something, haven't you?"

"I can't." Tears trembled in her eyes. At this sign of childishness, Wally recovered some of his composure. "Stop bawling and let me think, can't you?" he said roughly. "I've gotter think what to do." He sat down on the steps of the summer house, gazing sternly in front of him, his chin in his hands. His pose did not deceive Hilary.

"You can't do anything, you're only a boy," she accused.

"I'm bigger than you," he argued, hurt. "Besides, I've got a scholarship." For once, this fact did not help his self-esteem. "You've made it all up," he said, not believing this for a moment but unable to think of anything else to say.

"I didn't." Hilary licked her finger and drew it across her throat. "Cross my heart."

"You did."

"I didn't. Oh, you're no *good*," she screamed at him and ran round the side of the house. Wally sat, scraping at the earth with the heel of his boot, scowling fiercely. Then he got up, retreated a few yards and began to throw stones at the summer house. One of them cracked the small, dusty window and he glanced round guiltily, scarlet in the face. Thrusting his hands in his pockets, he followed Hilary. He found her, crouching by the front gate, a kitten in her lap. It was dead and covered with dust; its small head hung over her knee at an unnatural angle.

"Coo," he said, "where did you get that? You'd better put it down or you'll catch something. Germs," he ended impressively.

She looked at him coldly. She was not crying and this filled him with awe and admiration. "It's mine," she said and her mouth set in a thin, obstinate line. "It was in the hedge. *He* killed it and threw it there."

He knew to whom she referred. "Oh, come off it," he said concerned, and squatted down beside her. She stood up, the kitten clutched against her dress. "*You* . . ." she breathed contemptuously and, pushing past him, ran into the house.

The Fun Fair was crowded. At some of the resorts along the coast the fairs had closed down already and the car park was full of charabancs, motor-scooters and family cars. The dusty ground was covered with blowing paper; children buried their exultant faces in the pink glory of candy floss. Coveys of middle-aged women, squeaking like partridges, patrolled the ground wearing paper hats labelled Kiss-me-quick, Don't-look-now and Oh-boy-oh-boy. The lights were lit on the roundabouts and on the stalls; music blared from the Tannoy high above the Scenic Railway which towered like a neolithic skeleton against the dying sky.

Hilary, clutching her purse in the pocket of her frock, was filled with a wild and splendid happiness. It seemed a miracle that she was here at all, a piece of staggering luck. She did not connect it with the kitten's death. Once it was buried, decently coffined in a shoe box, beneath the laburnum bushes at the bottom of the garden, its death had ceased to trouble her. She had had plenty of pets and was accustomed to their dying: it was not nearly so painful as when they escaped from their match boxes or jam jars or, like the caterpillars, turned into butter-flies and flew away. But the grown-ups had surrounded her with sad and solemn faces, given her sweets and asked her if there was anything special she would like to do. "Such a dreadful shock for the child at this time," Alice had said in an undertone to Janet. Auntie had given her a necklace of moonstones in a Victorian silver setting to wear with her party dress. Hilary, bewildered by this sudden rush of attention, had not lost her head. She seized, without much hope, on the one concrete offer. "I want to go to the Fun Fair," she said in a whining voice. She did not expect her request to be granted—it came into the category of unattainable joys like the full-size bicycle or the pony she asked for every Christmas-time. But she did not show her astonishment when, after a hushed discussion she was told that she might go, just this once, and was given some money to spend.

Janet took her on the Scenic Railway. They climbed, on the creaking cable, to the top of the last, highest dip and rushed gloriously down through the pale, cold air, shrieking against the wind. Hilary saw the world turn and topple, change into fantastic shapes; she saw people with legs like pins and enormous, gaping faces. When they lurched into the wooden platform and the ride was over, she felt sick and her legs were trembling.

They played Bingo. Hilary was bored because only two of the numbers on her card came up but when the game was over and Janet abruptly left her seat, Hilary ran after her, shouting, "But I wanted another go."

"Then Want must be your master," said Janet in a cold, school-mistressy voice. Her unfriendliness sobered Hilary. She tugged at her sister's hand and gave her an ingratiating smile but Janet jerked her hand away and stared into the distance in an offended way.

"What's the matter?" asked Hilary in a fretful voice.

Janet gazed at her bitterly and said, "You stole my letter." Hilary was startled by the trembling anger in her voice. She could not remember the incident. She stared at Janet, open-mouthed, a stupid expression on her face.

"It was a beastly thing to do," continued Janet, two red spots appearing on her sallow cheek-bones, "a nasty, deceitful, sneaky thing to do." With each adjective, she gave Hilary's shoulder a little push. The child looked down at her feet, bewildered, her happiness temporarily destroyed by this manifestation of dislike. "And I have to drag you round with me," went on Janet, giving her another push. "It's poor Hilary, poor Hilary, never poor Janet." Her words increased her vindictiveness towards her sister.

"Poor Janet," said Hilary in a placating voice. "I'm sorry."

"You're not, you never are, nasty, spoiled little beast," said Janet viciously. Then her expression changed. She smiled. Surprised, Hilary saw the smile and essayed one of her own before she saw that Janet was not smiling at her but at Aubrey, who was coming towards them with long strides, his open, worsted jacket showing a brightly coloured, cotton shirt.

"There you are," he said, pressing Janet's hand and looking down at her lovingly. They walked across the fairground, talking in low tones. Hilary trailed after them. They stopped outside the Big Laugh.

Hilary said loudly, "I want to go into the Big Laugh. It's full of funny mirrors and it's a maze. Sometimes people get lost in there for days and days and no one finds them till they're dead and their bones are sticking out like matches."

"Silly child," said Janet indulgently and smiled upon her for Aubrey's benefit.

Aubrey said, "Why such a fat child should have fantasies of starvation bewilders me." Janet laughed, a high, ringing laugh as if he had said something surpassingly witty. The man in the pay box of the Big Laugh shouted, "Come along, ladies and gentlemen, see yourselves as you really are. In some cases, people find it an improvement."

"It's like another world," said Aubrey in his sad, parsonical voice, "not just a reflection of this one." He stared deep into Janet's eyes as he said this and Janet looked uncomfortable. He murmured something in her ear and, in the mirror, two fat midgets held hands. Hilary scuffed the toe of her sandal along the ground. A deep disappointment invaded her: nothing was ever so wonderful as she expected it to be.

"I want to go on the Roller Coaster," she groaned.

"It's too fast. It would make you sick. You were nearly sick on the Scenic Railway."

"I wasn't. Anyway I don't care if I'm sick. I want to go. More than anything in the world."

"The roundabout is better, dear." Aubrey smiled in a patronising manner and patted her on the head. "Look, see the horses. . . ."

She was perched high on a galloping horse with flaring red nostrils and golden stirrups. She clutched at the brass pole in front of her and the roundabout began to move. In the middle, a mechanical drummer banged his drum and nodded his head. The world flew past her, a mad panorama of colours and light: in the middle of the world, Hilary swooped and soared like a creature of the air. "Lovely," she screamed and kicked at her horse's sides. Briefly, she closed her eyes and it was like the moment of flying in a dream just before you wake.

The roundabout slowed down, the kaleidoscope pattern resolved into the Bingo table, the shooting gallery with the bobbing, white, cardboard ducks, the rolling balls where you got a prize every time and, high above them all, dominating and unattainable as age, the Big Wheel.

Then there was the Bingo table again and, standing beside it in a long, black coat, a thin and familiar figure. The next time round, the horizontal movement of the horse more noticeable now they were moving slowly, he was still there, his collar turned up round his chin, chewing at his nails. Hilary craned sideways to watch him as she was carried out of sight and almost lost her balance.

She slid off her horse and looked for Janet and Aubrey. They were waiting for her at the other side of the roundabout.

"I saw him," she said. "I saw the man who took the little girl away. He's watching Bingo."

Excited, she pulled at their reluctant hands, drawing them towards the Bingo and the lonely, watchful figure.

Their eyes, wide and disbelieving, turned towards the round stall with its arched canopy of striped canvas, its gaudy mound of prizes, stuffed dolls, whistling kettles, plaster cats. The man chanted the numbers in a syncopated rhythm. On the spot, number four; on the spot, eighty-two. . . .

"There, look . . ." Her voice was shrill and triumphant. The man looked in their direction.

"Hilary." Janet's face burned.

Hilary persisted, "It *is* the man. I know. I talk to him sometimes." She was not afraid, she was exhilarated. She pranced and capered round Aubrey and Janet, her face radiant with joy. "He's the Devil, the Devil, the silly old Devil, his jacket was red and his breeches were blue and there was a hole where his tail showed through . . ." She howled the last words in a paroxysm of delight.

Janet seized her by the shoulders. "*Do* be quiet," she hissed. "Oh—I could *beat* you."

Hilary twisted out of her grasp. Her eyes were bright and luminous, excitement twisted in her stomach. "He is, he is, silly Janet, soppy Janet." She turned in a pirouette, her cotton skirt flying round her. The man was gone.

"What newspaper do you take?" asked Aubrey. Janet nodded at him, her lips compressed into a disagreeable grin. Aubrey bent and said in a soft, mocking voice, "Hilary, Hilary, what a tangled web we weave, when once we practise to deceive. . . ."

Hilary screamed with laughter and butted him in the stomach. He caught her hands and swung her round in a wide circle. Sudden gaiety possessed them all. They walked, hands clasped, among the glittering stalls. Little puffs of dust blew in their faces. The colour had begun to fade out of the sky.

They went on the Ghost Train, jammed into the same, rattling carriage. Skeletons rose out of the dark, gleaming like dead fish, hands brushed their shrinking faces. They whirled out into the light through clashing doors. Hilary shouted, "Lovely, lovely, I wasn't frightened, I'm never frightened."

She went, alone, down the Helter Skelter, landing on the mat at the bottom, her skirt flying over her head. Her face scarlet, she rolled deliriously on the mat, dragging her skirt over her head. "I showed my knickers," she shouted, scrambling to her feet and running to Janet. "Whoopee."

She saw the yellow light winking in the distorting mirror. "I want to go in the Big Laugh."

"You've had enough. It's time to go home." Janet's hair was wild and tangled as a gipsy's, her skin glowed with colour. She was drunk as Hilary was drunk: this was life, happiness, not the sombre colours of death. She leaned her head against Aubrey's shoulder, loving him truly now she was going to leave him for ever, crooning a sentimental song. She felt the blood tingle along her veins, the glorious strength of her young body. "I'm going to London, to London town," she cried suddenly, and the world opened at her feet.

"Come on, come on," Hilary grasped their hands. They laughed.

"Go by yourself, then."

She ran, the turnstile clicked and she was inside. It was dirty with bright, glaring lights. The passages, lined with mirrors, twisted and turned.

Hilary was long and thin, her neck as graceful as a swan's. She turned sideways and smiled at herself. She was thin: perhaps when she grew up she would be thin like this and wear long, pink satin dresses and a spray of orchids on her breast. She would be a Princess. She bowed deeply to her reflection. "Your Highness . . . if Your Highness permits. . . ."

Someone moved in the mirror behind her, a giant, incredibly tall, incredibly thin. His dead eyes met Hilary's in the glass; she turned and the corner of his raincoat whisked round the corner.

Drawn, like a person in a dream, like a pin to a magnet, she followed him through the pattern of changing shapes. She had a feeling of fearful excitement, of awe, as if she were on the point of some essential discovery. There were hundreds of Hilarys, fat ones, thin ones—all with blue, cotton dresses and brown, sandalled feet. Then he was there too: in the mirrors his reflection flickered and changed until reality no longer existed. Only the opaque eyes and the long, bitten fingers, twisting in the mirror did not change.

"Hallo, Girlie," he said softly and smiled, showing his long, yellow teeth. His fingers closed on her shoulder, she could feel the heat of his hands through the stuff of her dress.

"Let me go," she cried, but the fingers tightened. She bent her head and bit his hand: it was like biting a bone.

He let go and she ran, with an enormous head and thin tapering legs towards the end of the passage. She put out a hand and it disappeared as she approached the glass. She slipped into another passage. She was tiny now, a tiny Hilary running in a blue dress down an empty corridor. Then the man was behind her, a fairy creature with legs made of pea sticks. She opened her mouth but no sound came out of it except a small, hurt whimper. She stumbled beneath the red Exit sign and out into the fairground.

It was getting dark now, the lights were brighter and there were more people. She looked for Janet and Aubrey but they had gone. Behind her, the man called in a coaxing voice, "Girlie, wait for me," and she ran past the Dodgems and the Bingo table, past the Ghost Train to the Enchanted Garden. She saw Janet and Aubrey in one of the moving trucks that took you through the Garden to the Blue Grotto where there was falling, coloured water, magical caves full of treasure and fairy lights among the trees.

She called, "Janet," but her voice was thin and small and lost in the noise of the fairground. To the accompaniment of Handel's Water Music, Janet and Aubrey were borne into the Enchanted Garden.

She ran on. She ran into a fat woman, hitting her hard in the middle of her stomach.

"Look out," said the woman, and caught her by the elbow.

"Please," she said. "Please," looking up into the kind, fiery face beneath the hat crowned with roses. For a moment she thought she was safe, held close to the sheltering stomach, but suddenly the man was there, saying, "Come here at once, dear, do what your Daddy tells you. . . ."

"But you're not," she said with incredulous surprise and then she saw the concern fade from the woman's face and knew there was no safety there. She ducked beneath the plump arm and ran.

She slid beneath the barrier of the Scenic Railway and jumped into the last coach as it moved off from the platform. Someone shouted behind her: she stared straight in front of her, clasping the bar, longing for the first, slow climb to end and for the rush downwards to safety.

It was dark at the top of the climb, the velvet night received them. The coach poised for a moment above the brilliant fair and then plunged with a howl down into it. The lights went past like ribbons, the jolt at the bottom threw her against the bar. They climbed up again and she kept her eyes on the shaking, juddering structure, not daring to look outwards into the fairground. Up and down they climbed and swooped, their screams rose above the grinding music. They rushed into the last, dark tunnel, unbelievably black, and out into the light.

A big man bent over Hilary, his chin covered with stubble.

"Now see here, I could give you in charge. . . ."

"I've got my money," said Hilary and dragged her purse out of her pocket. "I want another go."

She opened it and shook it on to her lap. The purse was empty.

"That's enough of that, I know all about *you*," the big man roared. "Get out of here." He lifted her out of the coach and dropped her on the platform like a dirty puppy.

"Listen," she said, plucking at his arm.

The people were filing into the coaches for the next ride. She saw Wally, wearing his old clothes again, getting into the front coach. "Wally," she screamed, and he turned, searching short-sightedly among the crowd. He felt slowly in the pocket of his trousers and put on his spectacles. The train began to move away from the platform. Seeing her at last, Wally waved. His eyes went beyond her, beyond the barrier to the thin, waiting figure. He stood up in his seat. There was a gasp from the big man, a gasp from the crowd. Then someone in the coach pulled him down again and the train moved slowly on, upwards into darkness.

"Let me wait for my friend," begged Hilary, but the big hand propelled her firmly towards the barrier. "Off you

go, lucky I haven't sent for a policeman," the man scolded
wearily, used to the children stealing rides. "Don't let me
catch you here again."

The man stood, waiting, in her path. She swerved, dodged,
ran towards the exit. She was purposeful now. She was not
afraid: all feeling had dried up inside her. She would get on
a bus and go home. The conductors on the buses knew her:
she would be safe with them.

The streets were dark after the fairground and almost
empty. The sea was far out and still. On the shingle, the
beached boats lay and beyond them the last light glimmered
on the long line of mud.

The pier stretched its jewelled finger towards the horizon.
As she approached the stop the waiting bus moved off,
changed gear, passed her small, waiting figure.

There was no one on the front. Beyond the pier the road
was empty, there were no houses. Only the shacks and the
marshes and the waiting sea.

As the Scenic Railway rattled and clattered and dived,
Wally sat, still as a stone statue in his seat, hunched over
the bar in front of him. Excitement raged within him.
He was not frightened, but thrilled, at the emergency
that had arisen. Life was at last living up to the promise
of the comic papers and the Telly. He, Wally Peacock,
was called upon to take heroic action. He muttered under
his breath, his gaze becoming fixed and purposeful. When
the train stopped at the platform he scrambled out hastily,
treading on the toes of the woman sitting next to him.
"Pardon," she called after him in an outraged voice
but he took no notice, merely making a hideous face at
her before he vanished beneath the barrier.

"Well," she said and turned, incapable of further speech
to the couple in the compartment behind her. They gave

her no support. Their faces, only a moment before con-
torted in wild, abandoned screaming, assumed their normal
blank surfaces. Their eyes stared beyond her with faint
reproach.

Wally could not see Hilary. He ran aimlessly round the
sideshows, pushing his spectacles more firmly on to his nose.
His initial feeling of purpose deserted him. He stopped at
the shooting gallery and watched a military man with a
moustache knock down the moving file of painted jungle
animals, one after another. Transfixed by this display of
skill, Wally stood with his mouth drooping open. The man
called for another turn and dug a handful of change out of his
pocket. A silver coin tinkled to the ground and Wally was
on to it like a terrier, running with bumping heart while the
man shouted half-heartedly after him. Hiding behind the
Haunted House, he examined his prize, a florin, with pride
and joy. Thrusting it into his pocket, he swaggered triumphantly through the fairground, a gay buccaneer on the
prowl.

"Wally." A boy hailed him from a waiting queue. "Come
on the Tubs."

Wally gave him a sneering, supercilious look. "That's jus'
kids' stuff."

The boy was faintly crestfallen but returned with spirit,
"Go on, now. You haven't got the money."

"I have," Wally answered, stung, and displayed his
wealth.

"Gawd, you must've pinched it." The boy produced an
insane, cackling laugh that was instantly echoed by his
buddies waiting in the queue.

Wally blushed. It was not the truth of this accusation
but the evidence of his own unpopularity with his fellows
that saddened him and made his response feeble. "I didn't,
so there," he said and, by some curious mental process

instantly recalled his mission. "I got better things to do than go in the ole Tubs," he said proudly.

"I got better things to do than go in the ole Tubs," chanted the boy triumphantly, and Wally knew himself to be beaten. Any retort he produced now, however cutting, would immediately be repeated: there was no satisfactory way to divert to your own advantage this well-tried method of defeating an opponent. Wally stuck out his tongue, turned his back and walked away. He reminded himself that there really was something important that he had to do. His anxiety mounted as he realised that he had no clear idea of how to do it—in his heart, he had expected his plan of rescue to be laid before him, as gloriously simple as something on the pictures.

He saw Janet and Aubrey watching the Dodgem cars. No particular worry was expressed on their faces. This diminished his own sense of urgency and made him unwilling to appear ridiculous. He went up to them and said, "Miss," in an almost inaudible voice. Janet turned, surprised. "Oh, Wally," she said kindly, "are you having a lovely time?"

Her condescending air annoyed him. "I'm looking for Hilary," he said nervously. Realising that this remark might have an arch significance, he flushed unhappily.

Janet smiled broadly and raised her eyebrows. "I expect you'll find her if you look hard enough, dear," she said in a grown-up voice.

Who does she think she is, he thought rebelliously. Only seventeen and acting like she was twenty.

He scowled. "She's scared," he said. "I saw her and she was scared."

"Couldn't find *us*, I expect," said Janet with an odd note of satisfaction in her voice. "Serve her right," she added suddenly and with a most un-adult nastiness.

Wally was so dumbfounded by this descent into childish spitefulness that his powers of reasoning were temporarily destroyed. He saw only that Janet "had it in" for Hilary and therefore did not care what happened to her. Two other factors contributed to this assessment of the situation. He believed that Janet understood as powerfully as he did the extent of Hilary's danger—it had been such an effort for him to approach her that he confidently expected her to realise at once the full urgency of his message. He was also disconcerted by the discovery that Janet was not properly "grown-up" and so could not be relied upon to act with real responsibility in the matter. He thought, with some justice, that she was a fool and he had a precocious contempt for fools.

He said, in an anguished voice, "You *oughter* do *something*. It's Dotty Jim. It's awful," and fled with a scarlet face.

"Looking for attention," said Janet in a superior voice, but her face and voice were uncertain.

"I think we should look for her," said Aubrey judiciously. "One doesn't know, it may be something important."

Wally ran, his expression serious and lowering. He called Hilary's name in a shrill, nervous voice. People turned to look at him briefly, attracted by his air of intense anxiety. Near the entrance to the Fun Fair, he saw a policeman and at once slowed down, halting a few yards away from the blue clad figure. His normal fear of the boys' natural enemy asserted itself. He had run, so often, from the Law, that he could not now approach with confidence. He remembered, with belated guilt, the florin he had stolen. Perhaps the man at the shooting gallery had told this very policeman, perhaps he was, even now, on the lookout for a fat boy in spectacles. Furtively, he removed his glasses and slipped them into his pocket.

The policeman appeared, through a fog of defective vision and terror, as an enormous man with a menacing air of authority. Wally's bladder weakened, he turned away, clutching his groin. Then Hilary's face rose up before him, freckled, pale, surrounded by a mass of floating hair. He hesitated, swallowed at the lump in his throat and then performed the most heroic action of his life. He went blindly up to the policeman and touched him on the arm.

As Hilary jumped from the promenade on to the beach, a stone spat up from the shingle and hit her knee. She fell, moaning, beside a boat: the man came down like a great, black bird and put his arm around her.

His voice was gentle and crooning. "Girlie, why did you run away from Uncle? I only wanted to show you something nice." A trickle of spit ran out of the corner of his mouth. "We'll have a lovely time, would you like some sweeties? I'll give you some if you come with me."

"I'll tell my Mummy." She wriggled and he let her go. One hand was hidden inside his raincoat.

"Don't be frightened of Uncle. I won't hurt you. Not a nice little girl like you. I only want you to have a nice time. At home I've got a walkie-talkie doll, wouldn't you like to come with me and see it?"

"You're a liar," said Hilary, coldly and precisely.

His voice chided her. "What an unkind thing to say to Uncle. Uncle only wants you to be happy. It's cold on the beach. Look at you, in a thin frock. Let's go back to the fair, you can go on anything you like and then I'll take you home, I promise."

His voice was kind and gentle. Calmed, Hilary thought of the Roller Coaster, even, perhaps, the Big Wheel.

She hesitated. He stood up and held out his hand to her.

"Come along. There's a nice, good girlie. We'll have a lovely time, won't we?"

The young moon shone like a pale ghost in the sky. He was lit with an unearthly radiance. She saw his hoof, his horns, the sad, beautiful face of a fallen angel. She was not in the least afraid. "I'll come," she said. "I promised I'd come, didn't I, to see your bird?"

Wally said, "But she's only little. Nobody listened to her. She's only nine."

The policeman had a round face like a balloon.

"Now, now, son," he said. "If you're having me on, there'll be trouble." His voice was threatening but there was comfort in it.

Wally shuffled his feet. "I'm not having you on, honest." His pale face gleamed earnestly. "Please," he said insistently, tugging at the uniformed arm, "please." He choked back a small, childish sob.

The policeman looked down at him. "You're not so big yourself," he said, smiling. In spite of his natural wariness where all boys were concerned, he was impressed by this one. Sharp-eyed, he saw the character behind the flabby cheeks, the unhealthy pallor. This was a brave boy and a good one.

"Come along then," he said kindly. "We'll go along to the station, shall we? Don't you run off, either," he added in a grim voice. It was only a formal warning; he knew that Wally would not run away.

They left the Fun Fair and came out on to the empty front. Beyond the string of fairy lights, the beach was dark.

"We don't know where they are," said Wally suddenly. "It'll be too late." And in misery and dreadful shame, he began to cry like a baby.

The man was going too fast. Hilary, clinging to his hand, was dragged along in his wake. When she stumbled on the shingle, her arm was nearly jerked out of its socket. She wanted to ask him to go slower but her breath was coming in great, panting gasps and she could not speak.

There was a light wind blowing off the sea. Hilary's feet were sore from the stones and the bruise on her knee was hurting her. They were walking some way away from the promenade and the darkness of the beach enclosed them. It seemed to Hilary that she and the man were quite alone, cut off completely from the world she knew.

She was not, however, afraid of him. She even felt a strange sense of security in his presence. His hand was hard and firm and comforting. She had forgotten where they were going and why, but she trusted him completely.

On their left, the lighted part of the promenade came to an end. The man stepped easily over the high, green breakwater, and helped Hilary up. She caught her toe on the slimy top and slipped, face downwards, on to the wet beach. Her face was cold against the cold stones, her heart pounded in her chest. She felt his gentle hands beneath her shoulders, he set her on her feet and she swayed against him.

"I'm tired," she complained.

He muttered something beneath his breath. Then, with a swift movement, he swung her up into his arms. She lay inert, her head against the rough stuff of his coat. He staggered beneath her weight, slipping on the uneven beach. He coughed, a fearful, racking cough that Hilary felt throughout her body.

"Put me down," she said, full of concern for him. "I'm much too heavy for you."

He did not answer her but changed his direction and

climbed awkwardly up the steep mound of shingle towards the promenade. He sat her on the concrete ledge and heaved himself up beside her, ducking beneath the bar.

"You can walk now," he said and, reaching down, clawed for her hand.

She shook her head obstinately. "I'm tired," she repeated almost angrily, "I want a little rest."

"No," he said violently and jerked her to her feet. He was shivering, either from fear or cold or both. He glanced quickly over his shoulder. "You're coming with me, d'you hear? You're coming with me."

"Of course I'm coming," said Hilary, annoyed. "But it's a long way to your caravan. And my legs hurt. I'm tired."

He twined his fingers in her hair and forced her head backwards. Then he let her go and began to whimper gently. The tears flowed in silver streams down his dirty cheeks. "Poor Jim," he blubbered, "no one loves poor Jim."

Hilary was fascinated by his tears. Her own eyes began to water in sympathy. "Don't cry," she said in an affected motherly tone. "It's all right. *I* love you. Look, here's my hanky."

She slipped her hand cosily into his and they began to walk towards the Downs, the man's shoulders bowed and shaking. A middle-aged couple, emerging from a side street, glanced at them curiously and hesitated before they passed on. Hilary was quite happy now they were walking slowly and her legs no longer ached. She began to sing a tuneless little song under her breath.

They came to the beginning of one of the tarmac paths that wound up over the Downs. Behind them, someone shouted and turning, Hilary saw a policeman pounding along the promenade towards them.

The man dropped Hilary's hand and began to run.

The police station was hot and steamy. White lights flared smokily against a white ceiling. The walls were painted bottle-green.

The chair Hilary was sitting on was too high for her and her feet began to prickle with pins and needles. Someone gave her a cup of tea in a thick, white mug. A lady policeman with hairs on her chin and a stiff, dark moustache, wiped her face with a flannel and clicked her tongue sympathetically when she saw the cut on her knee. She kept saying, "There, there, it's all right now, poor little girl."

Hilary edged away from the kind, fussing hands. Her head ached and she felt a little sick. From time to time, she closed her eyes.

Then Wally was there. She saw his face, on her own level, white and fat and curiously unfamiliar without his spectacles. She said, "But you can't see without your glasses," and he put his face close to hers and said, "Shut up, can't you?" His voice was cross but he took her hand all the same and held it tightly. The two children sat side by side, waiting, and the man leaned against the opposite wall and stared at them. He looked tired and ill and beaten; beneath the lank, long hair, his face was like a skull. Hilary thought: poor old man, why don't they give him a chair?

There was a long interval. From time to time, the door opened and the room was chilled by a draught of cold air. Hilary dozed, her head lolling against the green wall. She saw her mother come into the room with a policeman.

"Darling," said Alice in a husky voice. "My own darling little girl." She looked ugly and quite old. She was wearing an old raincoat flung on in haste over her sweater and skirt. "Tell me what happened," she said. "Tell Mummy."

"I was going to see his bird," said Hilary, enduring her embrace. She was tired and confused; she did not understand what they wanted her to say. She had tried to explain about the man before and no one had listened or seemed to care. Now she did not want to talk about him.

Alice stood up and said something to the policeman behind the desk. He said, "Yes, I'm afraid we must know, Mrs. Bray."

Alice knelt down again, her skirt sweeping the dusty floor. She said in a low awful voice, "Now, darling, you must be careful and tell me the truth. Did he *touch* you anywhere?"

Hilary was aware that this was an unpleasant question: the tone of her mother's voice, the breathing silence in the room, told her her so.

"He held my hand," she said, ashamed although she did not know why.

"He didn't hurt you?"

She shook her head. "I was going to see his bird. I promised I'd go." She remembered that she had broken this promise once before. She felt weak and tearful.

Alice's back shielded her from the rest of the room. There was a murmur of voices. Wally had gone from her side and she heard his voice, talking to the policeman. Then Alice spoke, the man behind his desk answered her. Hilary closed her eyes. The room seemed very far away, on the other side of a glass wall. Someone said, "The Devil—well, I never did," and there was a ripple of laughter. Looking up, Hilary saw Alice's hot, angry face, the skin stretched tight over her cheekbones. "She's not a liar," she said. "She doesn't tell lies." Her voice sounded sad and helpless and for the first time Hilary was sorry for her. It was quite a new feeling, strange and disturbing like the small, hard swelling she had recently discovered round her nipples. It made her want to cry.

There was a hum of voices. Wally's pale, accusing face swam in front of Hilary. "You told me he was the Devil," he said. "You told me."

"Well, he isn't," she said, flatly and rudely. "Aren't you silly? Can't you see he hasn't any horns, he hasn't got a tail?"

She was not quite sure how or why she had reached this new certainty. She only knew, quite clearly, that the man, with his poor, pale face and dirty clothes was not, and never had been, the Devil. It now seemed faintly embarrassing that she had believed any such thing. Her fears were far off and forgotten, she dismissed them as if they had never existed.

"Besides," she said crossly, "if he was the Devil, the policeman wouldn't have been able to catch him, would he?"

The actual circumstances of the man's arrest, which she had witnessed, had shocked her deeply and aroused in her the strong, sentimental loyalties of childhood. The man was her friend, he had been going to show her his bird and the policeman had knocked him down. She had forgotten that she had ever feared him.

"I never thought he *was*," said Wally indignantly. "You didn't half tell me a lot of lies, didn't you?"

He was hurt and angry. He had made what his mother would call "an exhibition of himself" and it was all Hilary's fault. He hated her.

"Oh, no, I didn't," she said in a clear, cross voice. "I told you he took Poppet away and he *did*. I saw him."

Suddenly there was silence. Everyone turned and looked at the two children. Hilary saw there was a new man in the room, one who had not been there earlier on. He was an old man, not a policeman. He was not wearing a uniform.

Someone said, "It was all in the newspapers."

"She read the paper," said Alice wearily. "I hoped she hadn't understood."

"This was something she didn't read in the newspaper," said the man in ordinary clothes. He came towards Hilary and crouched in front of her chair. "Hilary, will you come and talk to me?" he asked.

He had a nice face with blue, bristly marks on his chin. He smelt of cigars.

"All right," she said and stood up. The man was standing against the wall. There was a clear space all round him as if nobody wanted to be near him. He looked very sad and very lonely.

The new man took Hilary's hand and led her into a small quiet room. There was a desk and a bowl fire and a small rug in front of the desk. He sat her in a swivel chair and leaned on the desk, looking down at her.

"Hilary," he asked her, "do you tell lies?"

"Sometimes," she admitted cautiously.

"Big ones or little ones?"

"Only little ones." She was shocked. "People who tell big lies go to hell."

"Oh—we can't be sure of *that*, you know," he said quickly and kindly. "We can only be sure that they'll get into some kind of trouble sooner or later." His face crinkled as he smiled at her until his skin was covered with tiny lines like the outside of a nut. "You mustn't tell me even a little lie, now, because it is important. Why were you frightened of the man?"

"I don't know." She considered. "I thought he was the Devil. But he's not, is he, he's just a poor, old man?" A faint, very faint anxiety clouded her eyes.

"Yes, he's just a poor old man." He had stopped smiling now and his face was suddenly very sad. Hilary thought she had never seen anyone look so sad. "Whatever they tell you later on," he said, "you'll remember that, won't you?"

Hilary wondered what he was talking about. She said, "I don't expect they'll want to talk about him. They never wanted to listen, after all. I expect they were too busy. People usually are." She spoke in a flat, thoughtful voice, her eyes fixed on her dangling feet.

"*I'm* not busy now," he said.

She looked at him, without interest, and frowned. "I promised to see his bird, you know. It's wrong to break a promise, just as wrong as it is to tell lies. Can I go and see his bird to-morrow?" She spoke urgently, as if this were very important to her, and looked at him.

"I don't know. Sometimes promises have to be broken." He saw the rebellion in her eyes and added hastily, not wishing to upset her now, "Perhaps you can go. We'll see."

He saw that she accepted this, not because she believed him but because she had suddenly grown old enough to know that she had no alternative: she could despair, or she could allow herself to be soothed by a consolation that did not console. He also saw, fingering the bristles on his chin, that she was not really interested in him, nor in what he had to say to her. She was absorbed in a world of new discoveries: that other people are not to be relied upon; that promises can be broken; loyalty abandoned; the world that is also childhood's end. Then his expression changed. He was not concerned with the child, she was not his business. His voice became crisp and clear.

"Come now," he said. "Tell me how you knew the little girl was called Poppet."

And in a calm, disinterested voice, because the entire episode had ceased to have any meaning for her, she told him.

TITLES IN THE NEW WINDMILL SERIES

Erik Haugaard: *The Little Fishes*

Esther Hautzig: *The Endless Steppe*

Bessie Head: *When Rain Clouds Gather*

Ernest Hemingway: *The Old Man and the Sea*

John Hersey: *A Single Pebble*

Nigel Hinton: *Getting Free; Buddy*

Alfred Hitchcock: *Sinister Spies*

C. Walter Hodges: *The Overland Launch*

Richard Hough: *Razor Eyes*

Geoffrey Household: *Rogue Male; A Rough Shoot; Prisoner of the Indies; Escape into Daylight*

Fred Hoyle: *The Black Cloud*

Shirley Hughes: *Here Comes Charlie Moon*

Henry James: *Washington Square*

Josephine Kamm: *Young Mother; Out of Step; Where Do We Go From Here?; The Starting Point*

Erich Kästner: *Emil and the Detectives; Lottie and Lisa*

M. E. Kerr: *Dinky Hocker Shoots Smack!; Gentlehands*

Clive King: *Me and My Million*

John Knowles: *A Separate Peace*

Marghanita Laski: *Little Boy Lost*

D. H. Lawrence: *Sea and Sardinia; The Fox* and *The Virgin and the Gypsy; Selected Tales*

Harper Lee: *To Kill a Mockingbird*

Laurie Lee: *As I Walked Out One Mid-Summer Morning*

Ursula Le Guin: *A Wizard of Earthsea; The Tombs of Atuan; The Farthest Shore; A Very Long Way from Anywhere Else*

Doris Lessing: *The Grass is Singing*

C. Day Lewis: *The Otterbury Incident*

Lorna Lewis: *Leonardo the Inventor*

Martin Lindsay: *The Epic of Captain Scott*

David Line: *Run for Your Life; Mike and Me; Under Plum Lake*

Kathleen Lines: *The House of the Nightmare; The Haunted and the Haunters*

Joan Lingard: *Across the Barricades; Into Exile; The Clearance; The File on Fräulein Berg*

Penelope Lively: *The Ghost of Thomas Kempe*

Jack London: *The Call of the Wild; White Fang*

Carson McCullers: *The Member of the Wedding*

Lee McGiffen: *On the Trail to Sacramento*

Margaret Mahy: *The Haunting*

Wolf Mankowitz: *A Kid for Two Farthings*

Jan Mark: *Thunder and Lightnings; Under the Autumn Garden*

James Vance Marshall: *A River Ran Out of Eden; Walkabout; My Boy John that Went to Sea; A Walk to the Hills of the Dreamtime*

David Martin: *The Cabby's Daughter*

John Masefield: *The Bird of Dawning; The Midnight Folk*

W. Somerset Maugham: *The Kite and Other Stories*

Guy de Maupassant: *Prisoners of War and Other Stories*

Laurence Meynell: *Builder and Dreamer*

Yvonne Mitchell: *Cathy Away*

Honoré Morrow: *The Splendid Journey*

R. K. Narayan: *A Tiger for Malgudi*

Bill Naughton: *The Goalkeeper's Revenge; A Dog Called Nelson; My Pal Spadger*

E. Nesbit: *The Railway Children; The Story of the Treasure Seekers*

E. Neville: *It's Like this, Cat*

Mary Norton: *The Borrowers*

Robert C. O'Brien: *Mrs Frisby and the Rats of NIMH; Z for Zachariah*

Scott O'Dell: *Island of the Blue Dolphins*

George Orwell: *Animal Farm*

Katherine Paterson: *Jacob Have I Loved; Bridge to Terabithia*